SHOOTOUT
AT CASA GRANDE

When Marshal Tide Buchanan put outlaw
Charlie 'Wink' Rachman in the Yuma State
Penitentiary for the murder of Hank Carter,
he knew the badman would seek revenge.
Sure enough, within six months, Rachman
was out, and aiming for a showdown with
Buchanan. The arrival of Wink Rachman
and his henchmen provokes a bloodbath,
and with sweet Beth Carter taken as hostage
Buchanan and his young deputy are forced
to ride after the outlaws. Only guile and six-
gun skills would defeat the badmen and it
would all end in a bloody shootout at the
Indian ruins of Casa Grande.

SHOOTOUT
AT CASA GRANDE

SHOOTOUT
AT
CASA GRANDE

by

Jim Lawless

Dales Large Print Books
Long Preston, North Yorkshire,
BD23 4ND, England.

British Library Cataloguing in Publication Data.

Lawless, Jim
    Shootout at Casa Grande.

A catalogue record of this book is
available from the British Library.

ISBN   1-84262-126-2 pbk

First published in Great Britain 2000 by Robert Hale Limited

Copyright © Jim Lawless 2000

Cover illustration © Prieto by arrangement with
Norma Editorial

Published in Large Print 2001 by arrangement with
Robert Hale Limited

Dales Large Print is an imprint of Library Magna Books Ltd.

Printed and bound in Great Britain by
T.J. (International) Ltd., Cornwall, PL28 8RW

ONE

Judge Ed Payne couldn't be certain what it was that had dragged him befuddled and protesting from just about the best danged sleep he'd had in the fifty years since he'd married Agnes Smallbone. All he knew was his eyelids had creaked back over yellowing eyeballs, he's stared blearily and uncomprehendingly into an unfamiliar gloom for close on half a minute then, with a mighty effort, had wriggled his stiff legs to the edge of the bunk and let them slide over in the forlorn hope that their weight would drag him upright.

With his skinny legs dangling off the edge of the bunk, Ed found the makings in the pocket of the rolled jacket he'd used for a pillow and swiftly and expertly fashioned himself a cigarette. A match flared, was skilfully applied to the quirly without igniting the overlapping straggly moustache. Blue smoke swirled and eddied. Ed coughed, squinted through the haze at the high square of the window, figured he'd been roused maybe an hour before a cold dawn – and, as the bite of the strong tobacco began sharpening his dulled faculties, he set his mind to thinking.

The only things that could rouse an old man from a deep sleep were a bright light shining in his face or one hell of a loud noise. Ed trickled smoke, narrowed his eyes, gathered slippery, hazy remembrances and grabbed them with both hands before they wriggled out of his grasp.

Yeah, that was it – but not one noise, two of them, and both of them almighty loud bangs.

Ed Payne let it rest there, sucking on the quirly until the burning tobacco scorched his fingers, and all the while his big ears were close to twitching like an old hound dog's so hard did he listen. But the sounds that had disturbed him were not repeated. Outside it was too early for street noises; inside, all was silent.

Ed noted that last fact, mulled over it, got himself nowhere. Hell, dawn still hadn't broken, no reason for Tide Buchanan to be up and about and even if he was Ed wouldn't hear him, damn feller always did move as quiet as an Injun.

Still and all...

With a ragged sigh Judge Payne dropped the cigarette on the dirt floor, walked unsteadily over to the bars of his strap-steel cell and peered out into the lamplit passage. And, as his arthritic fingers hooked onto the cold metal, he stared pensively at the wooden bench against the far wall and the closed hardwood door leading out to the office and wondered what the hell it was had dragged him from his sleep and taken Tide Buchanan, Marshal of Gila Bend, Arizona, out into the cold, dusty street.

A gunshot. A door slamming.

Yeah, that was it.

Only thing was, he couldn't recall which of them had come first.

'That damn gunslinger Charlie "Wink" Rachman broke out of the Pen more'n a week gone. Him and a real poisonous 'breed owlhoot, name of Pedro Torres.' This was Spencer Hill talking, six in the morning and already aproned up and with his big square hands tilting a barrel onto its rim ready to be rolled down the alley at the side of his mercantile.

Marshal Tide Buchanan sighed. 'All right, Spence, who was it brought the news, went trigger-happy and spoiled my sleep?'

'Yours and the judge's,' Hill said, and grinned broadly. 'It was young Josh Santee. Got hisself the idea him carryin' the news to Sally Grey'll put him ahead of the field.'

'She appreciate him firin' off his pistol outside her bedroom window?'

'If you call pourin' a bucket of cold water over his head appreciation, then yes, I reckon she did,' Hill said, his bright blue eyes twinkling. 'Was still tiltin' his head to get the water out of his ears when he came over to tell me about Rachman. Seems a couple of his pa's waddies rode in after a night in Montezuma, said word about the break had come over the telegraph.'

Buchanan nodded, then touched the big storekeeper's shoulder. He stepped off the sidewalk and moved away from the mercantile, the high heels of his worn leather boots making walking awkward as he cut at an angle across the sloping, deeply rutted street, his dark eyes narrowed and busy. Tall, dark and whipcord thin, his movements were cat-like, his face lean of cheek and deeply tanned.

Wink Rachman had returned to Arizona after an absence of two years, and on the first night back had ridden into Silver Spur and clubbed his sister's husband to death

10

with a peeled log. Later, on that same dark night and still stained with the dead man's blood, he had ridden into town, got himself roaring drunk and put the fear of God into Gila Bend's young seamstress before she was able to scream loud enough for help to come running.

Unconsciously, the marshal hitched his low-slung Remington as he stepped onto the plankwalk alongside McMahon's saloon and watched a buckboard emerge from behind the cottonwoods at the far end of town, drag a plume of dust past him and, axle squealing, bounce around in a tight half-circle to draw up in front of the mercantile.

Reliable news, this time, Buchanan thought, knowing that Wes Lake, Tumbling S's wrangler, was renowned for his straight talking. For an instant he hesitated, then walked past Harry Pepper's bank and the neatly painted premises occupied by Sally Grey, trod gingerly past another closed door alongside which hung Judge Payne's brass shingle and behind which Agnes Payne, née Smallbone, simmered with a perpetual rage, then stepped down off the plankwalk and turned into the sweet-smelling livery barn.

A door creaked open. Frank Parker

11

emerged from his office, short, skinny, red galluses dangling, with straggly grey hair and piercing blue eyes in a face as brown and lined as a year-old apple. The old army scout launched straight into the attack.

'When're you lettin' him out, Tide?'

'You know I can't answer that—'

'Why not! Ain't you the town marshal?'

'Sure, but—'

'And ain't you got a man locked up in one of them strap-steel cells, a man more used to lockin' people up than the reverse?'

'Yes, but—'

'Well, hell, you heard Agnes flyin' off the handle at Josh Santee. Now, I may be wrong, but it seems to me that her abrasive manner's a thousand time's worse since you slammed old Ed in the calaboose, and seein' as how it was too damn bad to put up with in the first place, I—'

'You hear about Wink Rachman?'

Parker blinked, his toothless mouth agape. 'How's that?'

'Rachman broke out of the Yuma Pen, Frank. Now, I can't say for sure which direction he's headed, but if you'd kindly walk down the runway and get my horse saddled maybe I can do the job I'm paid for and go warn decent folk to expect trouble.'

Five minutes later, when Tide Buchanan had rolled and half smoked the first cigarette of the morning and was picking a shred of tobacco off his lip as he looked idly down the street to where Spencer Hill was helping the Tumbling S wrangler load stores onto the buckboard, Parker came back up the runway leading the marshal's big blue roan. There was a worried look on his face.

'That right about Rachman?'

Buchanan swung into the saddle, settled, eased the big horse around.

'According to young Josh Santee.'

'Always did figure the only reason he came back nosin' around his sister's spread was 'cos he had them skewed eyes of his on Harry Pepper's bank.'

'The thought did cross my mind before I lost count calculating how many people benefited from Hank Carter's sudden death.'

'Yeah,' Parker grumbled. 'And maybe if you'd enforce that ordnance about no guns inside town limits a man'd get a night's sleep 'stead of–'

'That'd apply to you, too, Frank,' Buchanan cut in. 'If you're right about Rachman, are you happy to set there waitin' for him and his owlhoot pard to ride into town with

13

that big Dragoon of yours locked in my safe?'

He watched the old-timer's eyes narrow as he mulled that one over, then swung the roan into the street. 'I'll talk to Lake,' he said. 'Josh most likely got it wrong.'

But as he cantered away from the livery and headed back down the street, Buchanan knew he was clutching at straws. Josh Santee was an intelligent kid, certain one day to take over the spread from his pa, Cole Santee. Riding into town and loosing off his six-gun was a damn fool thing to do, but that didn't mean he'd got his facts wrong.

Spencer Hill was sitting on the steps, a thin film of sweat glistening on his face as the sun poked its dazzling rim above the mountains ranged to the east of Gila Bend. Wes Lake was leaning against one of the buckboard's wheels, trickling smoke as he watched Buchanan's approach.

'You tired of peelin' broncs, Wes?' Buchanan said as he swung down.

Lake chuckled. 'Tumbling S's cavvy's been ready for a week or more, everybody knows that.' He trickled smoke, said, 'You thinkin' of throwin' young Josh in alongside the judge?'

14

'For what? Spreading rumours?'

Lake shook his head emphatically. 'Naw. The kid's right. Wink Rachman's out, and runnin'.'

'Which way?'

'Nobody knows that for sure, Tide,' Spencer Hill said. 'But a man in your position, the lawman responsible for gettin' him a life sentence in Yuma, what would be your best guess?'

Buchanan shook his head, his eyes deliberately blank. 'Everybody in Gila Bend heard Rachman shootin' off his mouth in court, threatenin' to get me for catchin' him, old Ed Payne for passin' sentence. But six weeks in the stiflin' heat of the Pen livin' on Mex beans and dry bread?' He shrugged. 'Could be enough to push Rachman towards the border.'

Again, the Tumbling S wrangler shook his head emphatically. 'He's Beth Carter's brother. Could be he's got his own plans for the Spur.'

Buchanan swore. 'He battered Hank Carter to death. And the man's unbalanced, everybody knows that. Brother or not, I can't see Beth gettin' herself mixed up with a man who's plumb loco.' Buchanan glowered at the storekeeper, then swung on

Wes Lake who was busy clambering up onto the buckboard's high seat. 'What else did those two Tumbling S rannies overhear?'

'Rachman and Torres already murdered again. Stole clothes, weapons, horses.' He settled in his seat, said, 'You heard of Johnny Gaunt?'

'US Marshal?'

Lake nodded, the slack traces draped over his gloved hands. 'Seems like he rode out after Rachman and that 'breed killer.'

'One man?' Hill said scornfully, heading for the shop door.

'Could be enough,' Tide Buchanan said. He pursed his lips as the buckboard moved away from the plankwalk, its dry bearing rasping, turned away to call after Hill, 'I'll be gone most of the day, Spence.'

'Sure, I'll feed the judge for you,' Hill said, grinning over his shoulder. 'And I'll make sure Agnes stays well away.'

The buckboard spun its half-circle. Buchanan raised a hand, yelled, 'Thanks, Wes,' then clicked his tongue and wheeled the big roan away from the mercantile and pointed its nose to the west.

As he rode out of town he thought about Wink Rachman and a 'breed called Torres. The easy ride for two prisoners on the run

16

from Yuma was along the Gila River, but the easy ride was what would be expected of them. That being the case, their choice would likely be the Gila Desert and the Mohawk Mountains to the south, then across San Cristobal Wash to come into Gila Bend from the south-west.

With any other man on their trail, Buchanan would have backed the outlaws to shake off pursuit. But Federal Marshal Johnny Gaunt had a reputation for hanging on like a dog to a bone, and for taking no chances. A bullet in the back from long range was one of the ways he finished off his quarry, and if the method didn't exactly sit easy with his superiors, they were more than happy with the results.

Maybe, Buchanan thought, that's already been done. More than a week since the break, Spencer Hill had said, and that was time enough for a man as coldly efficient as Johnny Gaunt. But as Gila Bend fell away behind the town's marshal and he headed towards the distant river and Beth Carter's Silver Spur, the thin, tuneless whistle that was meant to be sanguine had, even to Buchanan's ears, a decidedly hollow ring.

TWO

The first shot echoed flatly off the slabbed rock, the slug buzzing away like an angry hornet in the heat-haze. The echoes were still like the soft fluttering of insect wings against taut eardrums when Wink Rachman desperately spun his tired grey gelding and spurred it behind the nearest rock outcrop, his eyes already squinting up at the sun-drenched rimrock high above the far side of the canyon.

Pedro Torres was out of the saddle, a snake frantically wriggling on his belly towards the rocks as his horse trotted away with head high and stirrups flapping. Sunlight glinted on the pistol that had leaped into the 'breed outlaw's hand as he tumbled to the ground. Then dust spouted alongside his stovepipe boots and, as the distant gunman's second shot cracked, Torres cursed breathlessly and came up into a crouch to cross the remaining open space at a staggering run and fling himself down alongside Rachman.

'Remember how I done told you this was

a fine place for an ambush?' Torres gasped.

'But you didn't done tell me how we was supposed to avoid it,' Rachman mocked.

'That is because the best way I know would be to head in the opposite direction,' Torres said, eyes malevolent. 'We were within maybe a mile of the border. We could have crossed over, but no, you wanted to–'

'You're damn right I wanted to!' Rachman snapped. 'I've got unfinished business in Gila Bend, and no lawman sat on a ledge with a rifle is going to get in my way.'

'You see him?'

'I see his smoke, and that's all I need to finish him off,' Rachman said. He slid down from his horse, dragged a gleaming Winchester from his saddle boot and jacked a shell into the breech.

Torres grimaced. 'That is what Gaunt figured when he set himself up there to wait until we rode into the canyon – only, he was wrong.'

Rachman flicked a mildly interested glance at the 'breed outlaw. 'Johnny Gaunt?'

Torres shrugged. 'There was much talk on the chain-gang, before we made the break. The others, they told me. You make it, Torres, they said, they'll send Marshal

Johnny Gaunt out to bring you back belly-down.'

'We'll see about that,' Rachman said easily. 'See how he likes a taste of his own medicine.'

The outcrop behind which they were sheltering was high enough at its inner end to shelter a man on horseback, but sloped jaggedly out to the canyon floor. Rachman moved along it at a crouch, then straightened swiftly, poked his head over the rock and flicked a glance upwards. At once, splinters flew as a slug howled into the hot air and the distant rifle cracked. Rachman eased down, spat dust, said softly, 'He ain't moved. So all's I need now is one clear shot.'

Torres rolled onto his back, scanned the rocky canyon wall. He said, 'You are some sort of expert with that long gun, *compadre?*'

'If I can see it, I can kill it,' Rachman said softly.

'*Bueno.* There is a way up to that ledge, scrub oak for cover when you get there. If I had a rifle to keep his head down....'

'Pistol'll do,' Rachman said. 'All I need is him occupied.'

He left Torres and began clambering over loose boulders, making for the canyon wall where a wide, jagged crack concealed him from the rimrock and formed natural steps up to the high ledge of stunted scrub oak.

Pedro Torres removed his black Stetson. Greasy black hair tumbled over his forehead as he ripped a branch from a mesquite bush. He drew his six-gun, then used the branch to poke his hat around the low edge of the rock. At once, the distant rifle cracked. The slug clipped the hat. It spun crazily. With a jerk of his wrist, Torres flipped the mesquite branch. The hat leaped high, then flopped into the dust. As it hit the dirt Torres stepped to one side, popped up over the rock and blazed three fast shots with his six-gun at the rimrock then dropped back.

Behind him, stone clattered as Rachman disturbed loose rock.

Torres stretched out a foot and retrieved his hat. He planted it on his head, called, 'How are you making out, *compadre?*'

'Close.' Rachman's voice was fainter, breathless. 'Give me thirty seconds … draw him out again … and we've got him.'

Torres started counting, spat, took off his hat, looked at the bullet hole in the rim. He twisted his head to glance back at the canyon wall, his eyes glittering when he saw the flash of metal on the Winchester's barrel as Rachman wriggled onto the ledge.

21

Fifteen seconds.

Torres poked the mesquite branch into the crown of his hat. His lips moved as he counted off the seconds. Then, very slowly, he lifted the hat so that it showed above the rocks and began to crawl, moving the decoy along at a slow walking pace.

The distant rifle cracked, then cracked again. The first slug hissed over Torres. The second clipped the mesquite stick inside the hat, knocked it sideways, almost tearing it from Torres's hand. He gritted his teeth, hung on, held the hat steady.

Then, from the high ledge of stunted scrub oak, Wink Rachman fired a single shot.

The slug made a soft whirring sound in the hot air at it ripped through the haze and winged its way towards the distant gunman. With a grunt of utter satisfaction, Torres turned his back to the rock, slid down, removed the hat from the branch and sat listening. High above, a redtail hawk cried. Its shadow swept across the waiting 'breed. He lifted his black eyes to follow its flight, grinned savagely as he used his forearm to wipe sweat from his dark, unshaven face.

'Hey, Torres!' Wink Rachman yelled.

'You get him?'

'Put it this way. If you want a rifle to go with that pistol you stole, there's a feller up on the rimrock got no more use for his.'

On the long, dusty ride out from Gila Bend to Silver Spur, Tide Buchanan let his eyes roam free looking for a sight of the escaped owlhoots in the distant, shimmering heat haze, while at the same time his overheated mind took off to run in circles figuring out how this latest problem would add to Beth Carter's troubles.

Hank Carter's Silver Spur ranch had always been the poor neighbour to Cole Santee's massive Tumbling S, but the smaller ranch's location five miles upstream on the Gila River had long been a source of irritation to the big rancher.

A man couldn't raise cattle in Arizona Territory unless he had access to water, and the Gila and its tributaries was just about the only source of that precious commodity in the whole territory. The Hohokam Indians had succeeded in farming some distance from the river by constructing a seventeen-mile irrigation canal out to Casa Grande. But that had been so far back in time the only monuments to their labours were gullies overgrown with chaparral and

23

the ruins of a four-storey adobe dwelling. Nowadays there wasn't much sense going to all that work when there was land aplenty in the wide, fertile strip along both banks of the river.

Santee and Carter had both reached that sensible conclusion, but there were two good reasons why Cole Santee's blood-pressure soared at the mere mention of Silver Spur. The first was that Hank Carter had sort of sneaked onto the Gila when Santee's head was turned the other way, and once he got himself established it became clear that he was a far better drunk than he was a rancher. More than once he had allowed the bloating carcasses of long dead steers to pollute the waters of the Gila – and the Tumbling S had a thousand head of cattle that watered downstream.

The second reason was that Cole Santee was land hungry. Not hungry in the sense that he had a healthy interest in seeing his own spread expand, but hungry as in downright greedy: if another man had land, Santee wouldn't rest until, one way or another, he had taken it from him.

Like Wes Lake had told Buchanan – unnecessarily, as it happened – Santee had been close to talking Hank Carter around to selling Silver Spur. But with Carter dead, Beth had dug in her heels, stuck out her strong, stubborn chin and sent Santee packing.

And that, Tide Buchanan thought ruefully, was like waving a red rag in front of a mighty big bull. In the couple of months since Carter's death Santee had already made his move, first riding on the Spur to offer the same terms he'd more or less agreed with Beth's husband, then openly threatening the feisty young woman.

Beth was too proud to make a formal complaint to Marshall Tide Buchanan. Along with her sixteen-year-old son, Danny, and the couple of waddies making up her winter crew, she was sitting tight and courageously calling Santee's bluff. But now Wink Rachman was out. And Buchanan suspected that if the dispute between Tumbling S and Silver Spur had so far done nothing worse than smoulder and raise an unpleasant stink, the return of Hank Carter's killer could be the wind of change that would fan those embers into flame.

Midday. The sun was a ball of fire almost directly overhead, the breeze that had cooled Gila Bend before dawn a tantalizing memory. Just about baked all the way through, Buchanan pulled into the meagre shade of a lofty saguaro, fumbled his canteen out of his saddle-bag and took a long swig of lukewarm water. Then, narrowing his eyes against the glare, he rolled a smoke, swung out of the saddle with the quirly in the corner of his mouth and poured the rest of the water into his hat so that the roan could wet its throat.

A smudge of dust hung in the hot, still air, almost on the horizon. Buchanan watched it, trickled smoke; automatically glanced to where his Winchester was tucked under his saddle fender.

There was no breeze – but the dust was moving. Drifting south to north, which suggested whatever was lifting it was heading on a course that would intersect his own westerly line maybe a mile ahead. Could be Rachman, and the 'breed, Torres. If it was, Buchanan reasoned, the course they were riding to cut across his own would surely take them to Silver Spur.

He spent five minutes watching the drifting dust, saw it take form, saw the two black dots, a little way apart, at the head of the crawling yellow plume. And knowing that if they held that course – whoever the hell they were – they would be riding stirrup with him in a few short minutes, Buchanan mounted up, leaned down to loosen the Winchester in its leather boot, then moved out of the saguaro's shade and proceeded on his journey.

Desert gradually merged into coarse grass, the land falling gently to the richer pastures ahead with the cool scent of water in the air that caused the roan's ears to prick, its head to lift, its pace to quicken. So, no more than a couple of miles to Silver Spur, Buchanan reckoned – about the same distance to Santee's Tumbling S if he chose to veer a little way south.

And now the two riders trailing their plume of dust across the flank of the Gila Desert were level with him. But instead of holding their course they had turned and were now hammering west at a steady, mile-eating pace, their horses – even from Buchanan's position maybe three-quarters of a mile distant – glistening in the harsh light, clearly lathered and wrung out, but being pushed relentlessly.

No sensible rider treats his horse that way, Buchanan mused. No sensible rider crosses the Gila in the heat of the day unless he's chasing, or being chased....

Because he was looking in that direction

27

he saw the muzzle flash before he heard the crack of the rifle, saw the flash of sunlight on the barrel before he felt the wind of the shot.

A second shot followed the first; a third winged after it to kick up dirt under his mount's hooves. Then, as Buchanan tightened his lips, reached his decision and flicked the reins to send the eager roan into a full gallop towards Silver Spur, faintly to his ears, above the pounding of hooves, there came the sound of laughter.

Stretched out along his horse's neck, its flowing mane in his face, he turned his head. The two riders had not changed course, nor had they slowed their pace. The crazy laughter was gone, swallowed in the drifting dust. Again the sun flashed on a rifle barrel, but no shots followed and Buchanan guessed the weapon was being pouched, the gunman done with his wild shooting.

He had time to speculate again on where they were heading, decide somewhat lazily that the direction they were riding would see them cross the Gila midway between Tumbling S and the Silver Spur which, if nothing else, meant that Harry Pepper could breathe easy when he locked the bank for the night, and Beth Carter was safe. Then, as if to mock his thoughts, the faint crackle of gunfire came to Buchanan's ears. But this time it was from far ahead, carried on the faint, cooler turbulence coming off the river.

Never mind Wink Rachman and his owlhoot pard, Buchanan thought, gritting his teeth and raking the roan's flanks with his spurs – there was already trouble at Silver Spur.

THREE

Beth Carter's Silver Spur spread was set back from the Gila and separated from its waters by a broad stand of healthy grey cottonwoods that stretched for half a mile along the river in either direction. Against those trees and nestling in a hollow, the ranch buildings – house, barn, bunkhouse – were solid timber structures erected by Hank Carter in the ten years since he moved with the young Beth to Arizona Territory. They were just about the only good things Hank Carter had bequeathed to his wife from a life that had been short and mostly worthless. Those, and young Daniel, who at sixteen was as lean and as hard as his pa but with none of the mental weakness that had been Hank's undoing.

But it was that mental toughness allied to supreme confidence in their own ability that was the undoing of countless Western youngsters and, as Tide Buchanan hammered in out of the Gila Desert then eased the roan back to cross a wide yard that reeked of gunsmoke and lathered horse flesh, he had a hunch that the shooting he had heard would have been of Daniel's doing, but would have done the youngster precious little good.

For if Cole Santee had come offering his hard cash for Silver Spur, he would have brought along tough men with guns to lend weight to the threats that were sure to follow hard on the heels of Beth Carter's flat rejection.

Three riders were bunched in front of the house. Drawn weapons glittered in the sun. Snorting horses backed and turned, feeling the palpable tension in the hot air and drawing curses from their riders who were having a hard time keeping them under control. But not, Buchanan sensed, as hard a time as they were having dealing with Beth Carter. He rode up fast, deliberately making a show of his approach in order to draw the men's attention, in a sweeping glance took in Danny Carter, down on his knees on the house's gallery clutching a bloodied shoulder. Behind him, standing over the boy so that her knees were against his back, Beth Carter was glaring at the three men over the barrel of a Remington 10 gauge, her blue eyes blazing defiance.

'All right,' Buchanan called, 'it's over.' He spun his horse hard in the dry dirt to emphasize his words, let his vest slip back so that the sun glinted on the badge pinned to his shirt, let his right hand drift to his holster.

'The hell it is,' growled Cole Santee.

He was big and dark and overpowering, the Tumbling S owner, an immense hulk of a man with a huge ego and the conviction, always, that right was on his side. Most of the time, it was. If others didn't see it that way, he used his power to convince them. If the power of his will was insufficient he could call on the power of money, as he had done successfully with Hank Carter. Against Beth Carter's sheer cussedness he would be wasting his time with both methods, and he knew it. So now, flanked by Matt Oakes and Vince Raper, he was using brute force, and it was the Tumbling S strawboss, Oakes, who was holding the six-shooter.

'I say it is,' Buchanan repeated. 'You don't agree, well, it's a long hot ride to Gila Bend and an empty cell.'

The tow-headed strawboss laughed, pale-blue eyes dancing, white teeth flashing under his drooping dragoon moustache.

'Yeah,' he said, 'I heard you'd taken to lockin' up old men.'

He ignored the black look Santee threw in his direction, went on easily, 'We rode in to talk, Tide. The kid stepped out of the house, pulled a gun.' He shrugged.

'Damn right I did!' Danny Carter said hotly, and Beth's hand came down, rested on his crisp, curly hair, holding him to silence.

'And now I'm toting a shotgun,' she said in a small, tight voice, 'with both hammers cocked, so what are you going to do about that?'

'Ordinarily,' Matt Oakes said, 'a weapon like that'd cause me to back off. But like I said, ma'am, we've got talkin' to do.'

'Cole Santee wants to buy Silver Spur,' Beth Carter snapped. 'All right, I'm telling him it's not for sale.'

'That should be plain enough,' Buchanan said. He glanced at the woman's flushed face, said quietly, 'I guess it was Oakes shot your boy. You want to press charges, Beth?'

Santee snorted. 'You're not listening, Marshal. The Carter boy pulled a gun, fired the first shot. That's the start. As for the rest, just about everybody knows Hank Carter had agreed to sell.'

33

'Hank Carter's dead,' Buchanan said, and saw Beth Carter shiver.

'That's right.' Santee nodded. 'And now his killer's on the loose and before we know it–'

'Santee,' Buchanan said tightly, 'I suggest you ride out of here before your mouth gets you into trouble.'

'Damn you, Buchanan, you've no right–'

'Tide?' Beth Carter cut sharply across the Tumbling S boss, her voice strained, a fresh alarm in her eyes. 'What does he mean about Wink?'

'He means your brother broke out of the Pen, ma'am.' This was Vince Raper, black of eyes and visage, lean and unshaven, his voice gentle but deceptively so because, as Buchanan knew well, this man was the bad apple in the Tumbling S barrel. The lean gunslinger seemed unsurprised by the news of Rachman's break out, and for a moment Buchanan wondered about this. Then he shrugged the thoughts away as Raper finished, 'We all know the first place Wink'll head.'

'No!' Beth shook her head. 'No,' she said vehemently, 'you're wrong, Wink can't be free, *mustn't* be free...' She looked wildly about her, her fingers tightening in her son's hair so that he winced, reached up to grasp her hand. 'Even if he is,' she went on, her voice dropping until the listening men were forced to strain their ears, or miss the words, '…even if he is, he'll not come here – because he knows that if he does, I'll kill him.'

Santee sneered, 'Not you, my dear, because isn't a villain of Wink's calibre just what you need?'

'A villain to fight a villain, is that what you mean?'

'I mean a man who's already been accused of rustling…'

'Enough!'

There was a new bite to Tide Buchanan's words. Without waiting for a reaction he kneed his horse forwards until he was among the three Tumbling S men, jostling Oakes, forcing the tough foreman's mount to give ground.

'Put up your pistol, Matt, then you and Vince turn around and ride.' He saw Oakes hesitate and glance questioningly at Santee, at once swung on the Tumbling S boss and in an attempt to divert the man's anger said, 'As for you, Santee, I suggest you pay more attention to what goes on in your own house. First thing: your son's caused trouble in town. By rights, I should lock him up.'

Santee's jaw jutted. 'The boy's of age, what he does is his business and I'll back him to the hilt. Besides, from what I hear all he was doing was taking the bad news to Sally Grey.' He smiled, but the dark eyes were ugly. 'You were elected to that office you hold to deal with hard cases, not feisty youngsters. Or has Wink Rachman got you cowed?'

'Rachman rode straight on past here not thirty minutes ago,' Buchanan said, and heard Beth Carter's small gasp of relief. 'Which brings me to my second point. As far as I could tell' – and here Buchanan had no compunction about bending the truth – 'Wink and his owlhoot pard were heading fast for the Tumbling S.'

'Goddamn!'

Beneath his thick brows, Santee's dark eyes now narrowed with anger. He cast a final, baleful glance at the woman on the gallery, barked a command, then wheeled his horse and spurred it towards the gate. With deep irony, Matt Oakes flicked a gloved finger against the brim of his hat to Beth Carter, nodded towards Buchanan then rode after Raper and his boss. Within seconds, the three men were out of sight as they cut along the river where it curved north beyond the cottonwoods. The only reminder of their presence was the settling pall of dust and the blood staining the front of young Danny Carter's shirt.

Buchanan slid down from the roan, flipped its reins loosely over the tie-rail and took the steps up to the gallery in two long strides.

'OK, feller,' he said, 'let's get you inside.'

But Danny was already up and turning away, boots scuffing on the boards as he brushed aside his mother's restraining hand and bent awkwardly to pick up his six-gun from against the wall of the house.

'I couldn't stop him,' Beth said, the shotgun drooping, her eyes searching Buchanan's face. 'I was in the kitchen. He heard the horses coming across the yard, came out of the house and before I'd dried my hands, it was all over. I heard the gunfire....' She swallowed. 'Shouldn't you … shouldn't you be riding after Wink?'

Buchanan touched her shoulder, tried to take the shotgun and felt her tighten her grip, gave up and turned her gently towards the house. 'Let's get Danny fixed up.'

'That's avoiding the question, Tide.'

'And, as I recall, it wasn't exactly a straight

answer you gave Cole Santee.'

She whirled on him in the doorway, her face flushed. Danny slipped past her and went inside, muttering under his breath. Beth was breathing hard, her bosom rising and falling with the strength of her emotion.

'Tide Buchanan, you have no right to criticize me over anything I say or do to protect my property from men you are either too frightened of to oppose, or so subservient to you'd never risk putting your job on the line.'

The small scar over her left eye gleamed white against her natural tan and the flush of her anger. The mark of Hank Carter's drunken rage and hard, indiscriminate fists, Buchanan remembered; the mark – or just one of the many, physical and mental – that had destroyed Beth's love for the man she had married.

Buchanan had visited her many times in the past year, made his growing affection for her clear in subtle ways without ever stepping over the line between decency and disrespect while Hank was alive.

But now Hank was dead – and this still wasn't the time. Beth's fists were clenched, her eyes at once hurt, angry, and uncertain. And knowing that nothing he said now could do anything other than damage, Buchanan wisely held his tongue.

He shrugged, took a deep breath. 'Look after Danny,' he said softly. 'If you think he needs a doctor…'

She shook her head. 'The bullet grazed his ribs. I can cope.'

'Yes.' He wanted to reach out, touch her. Instead, like Matt Oakes, he touched the brim of his hat and turned away.

He was astride the big roan when, still standing somewhat forlornly in the doorway, she called, 'Are you riding to Tumbling S, Tide?'

'After Wink?' He twisted in the saddle to watch her as the impatient horse turned a full circle, saw the flicker of pain in her eyes and shook his head.

'I've got business in town, Beth.' He hesitated. 'What did Santee mean, about you needing your brother, a man already accused of rustling?'

'I have no idea.'

Buchanan nodded slowly. 'We'll talk again.'

Perhaps, he thought as he cantered out of the yard, the next time there would be even less warmth between them. Like it or not, as a lawman he was duty bound to go after

Rachman, and that duty was reinforced by personal reasons for wanting Wink Rachman locked up: pangs of conscience that, for the most part, Buchanan kept under wraps.

But if Wink Rachman hadn't been riding to the Tumbling S – then where in hell was he heading?

FOUR

They crossed the Gila River at the sweeping north loop some ten miles east of Montezuma, clattering across the stony ford with water splashing high and glistening, then heading towards the wide low country between the Eagle Trail and Gila Bend Mountains.

According to Wink Rachman, there was an old man, name of Chug Austin, who'd worked the foothills ever since being driven off the Gila by Mexicans out hunting Apache and taken in by Austin's dark skin, long hair, and his penchant for wearing a filthy scarlet bandanna as a headband. That, Rachman told Torres, had been back in the days of Santa Anna and his war against the United States. Austin's mind had been poisoned somewhat by the experience, so that for the past thirty odd years he had welcomed strangers the way a suckling doe greets a hungry cougar.

'Maybe,' Torres had said cautiously, 'we would be better off taking our chances with the law in Gila Bend,' no doubt figuring that if the old man saw them coming and took off into his mountain fastness, they would be like a couple of ducks sitting to be picked off by his big buffalo gun – about which Rachman had also been highly descriptive.

'We set long enough he'll get hungry and come down,' Rachman had replied without concern. 'And with a man like that, knows every inch of the territory, there ain't no finer place for us to hole up.'

They were just about the last words he had spoken, for round about then Torres had spotted the rider matching their course at a distance and decided that it was time he tested the fine rifle he had taken from Marshal John Gaunt. He'd got off two shots before the sharp-eyed Rachman had recognized the distant rider's big blue roan and kneed his horse in close enough to slam the rifle barrel so hard with his fist Torres came close to putting a bullet through his own foot.

The shock of the blow cut off Torres' crazy laughter, and a sullen silence ensued. It lasted fifteen miles, close on two hours according to Rachman's reckoning, as he squinted up at the sun and swung his labouring bronc off the easy slope they had been climbing and pointed it towards the high country. And that distance from the Gila, surely, put them mighty close to Chug Austin's hideaway.

'Jesus!' Torres said, almost groaning when he looked at the high slopes riven by deep-cut canyons.

'You've got it,' Rachman said, grinning. 'Feller in the Pen called Jesus Peña put me on to old Chug. Said he'd holed up with him ten years back. Even drew me a map.'

'I have seen no map,' Torres growled.

'In here.' Rachman tapped his forehead, then turned his attention to nursing the desperately weary grey gelding over rough ground that sloped steeply upwards through sparse clumps of ragged chaparral and manzanita but still showed signs of some use as a cattle trail.

Which fact Rachman filed away for future reference. Hell, he thought, a man can't ever outguess fate, figure out in advance what might turn out so darn useful it saves his life.

They followed that faint trail for another mile, while the sun beat down like a hot dead weight on head and shoulders and the dust of their passing was a thick yellow pall over the tortuous ravines and gullies.

Rachman pushed on hard, aware of the clatter of hooves fading as Torres dropped back to keep his sweating countenance out of the dust, but even more aware of the high ridges topped by stands of pine and spruce which afforded fine vantage points for an old man with a long rifle.

Then, abruptly, the two men rode out of a widening arroyo, topped a rise and found themselves on a grassy plateau surrounded on three sides by steep wooded slopes. The rattle of hooves became a muted thudding. The smell of woodsmoke was in the air and, as they rode past the mouth of a short box canyon, Rachman saw a line of fresh-cut brush piled across its mouth to create a natural pen, heard the soft lowing of cattle; thought he saw a flash of red where smoke rose like a streak of white paint into the blue skies and the scent of burning wood was sharply seasoned by a smell with a stronger bite.

Bridle metal jingled as Torres moved abreast of Rachman.

'Burning hair. Someone is making good use of a runnin' iron,' he said, and Rachman nodded, thinking back to the faint cattle sign and wondering if they'd ridden into the wrong camp.

Then they had crossed the meadow and in front of them, set back dark against the trees, there was the cabin he had heard described to him by a man who was doing life in Yuma, and the horses were pricking their ears and picking up the pace as cool shadows invited and a jumble of rocks beyond a patch of lusher, greener grass suggested the presence of pure water from a mountain spring.

Then even that luxury was forgotten as an angry shout rang out and, from the mouth of the canyon, a man came hammering towards them on a threadbare mule he guided with his knees because both his hands were occupied keeping a steady bead on the intruders with the long buffalo gun that flashed in the sunlight.

The shadows of evening were crawling across the desert when Tide Buchanan rode into Gila Bend and tied up in front of the jail. Across the street the windows of Spencer Hill's mercantile glowed warm. Light spilling from McMahon's saloon was already outshining the hazy sun, the half-dozen or so horses standing at the hitch-rail in front of Jake Orr's gin mill hip-shot and dozing.

There was also a light in Sally Grey's window, and Buchanan knew, sooner or later, he would need to pay her a visit. But travelling in that direction left him wide open to a tirade from the ever watchful Agnes Payne, and with a tightening of his lips Buchanan slammed open the heavy door and stomped into his office.

'How's it going, Ed!'

In answer to his call a throaty chuckle drifted through the open door of the passage leading into the cell room.

'Peaceable,' Ed Payne shouted.

Buchanan smiled tiredly. He unbuckled his gunbelt, hung it on the peg, took a few moments to slam the coffee pot onto the hot stove and roll and light a cigarette. Then, letting go a stream of smoke with a contented sigh, he flexed his shoulders and strolled through to his prisoner.

'Peaceable, meaning Spence managed to keep Agnes away.'

'Agnes is a God-fearing, church-going Christian lady who would experience a fatal attack of the vapours if she was forced to step inside a jail,' Ed Payne said, grinning through the strap-steel bars.

'Is that right?' Buchanan sat on the wooden bench facing the cells, trickled smoke, his eyes amused. 'I might just go get her.'

'It'd sure be the easy way out of this mess.' The judge eyed Buchanan's dust-caked clothing, the signs of weariness under his eyes and the limpness of his long frame, and said quietly, 'You talk to Beth?'

'And Cole Santee, and his pistol-happy straw-boss. All that about five minutes after gettin' shot at by Wink Rachman or his crony.'

'The hell you say!'

'Who else could it be? Only thing I can't figure is where the hell the two of them was heading. They came out of the desert, turned like they were makin' for Silver Spur but rode straight for the Gila.'

'Aiming to lie low till they're good and ready.' Payne nibbled at his grey moustache with his jutting lower lip. 'Harry Pepper dropped in, chewed the fat some. Told me he heard Josh shootin' up the dawn, knew straight off what it meant.'

'His bank's safe. Forewarned is forearmed – right, Judge?'

'Maybe. But you need a deputy. You've been playing a lone hand too long, Tide.' He grinned suddenly. 'I always was a mean hand with a shotgun. More than one feller's

47

been happy to see me ride over the skyline when he's been in a tight spot…'

'Days gone by, Judge.' Buchanan smiled to sweeten the bitter truth, said quietly, 'Spencer Hill's competent, and happy to do the job without a badge. If Rachman plays rough, he'll ride with me while Gay minds the store.'

'A man doing a favour's one thing, but if he's running around chasing bandits without pay his wife might raise some heated objections.' The judge let that sink in, then said, 'I could swear him in for you, Tide.'

'I know you could.' Buchanan dropped the cigarette, ground it under his heel. 'But if it comes to a raid on the bank, I'll need a posse not the owner of the town's general store.' He rose from the bench and turned to go, said, 'You eaten, Judge?'

Payne nodded. 'Spence made sure I packed enough away so's there's no chance of me slippin' between these bars.'

'He always was a crafty bastard,' Buchanan said. 'Maybe I'll talk to him about that badge – but first, some hot coffee.'

He went through to the office to the fruity sound of Ed Payne's chuckle.

And came to an abrupt halt.

'Shootin' holes in a fading moon is one

48

thing, Josh,' he said softly, 'but I don't take kindly to a man walkin' into my office and throwin' down on me with my own pistol.'

'That about sums up the way I feel about a lawman leaves helpless citizens unprotected.'

The voice was far from steady, the Remington cocked and unwavering. Josh Santee was a miniature replica of his father without the weight or the arrogance. Black hair poked from beneath a battered Stetson. Faded denims hung on hips as lean as a fence post. A worn gunbelt carried an old Colt Paterson with a broken grip. The eyes under the black brows he had inherited from Cole were, Tide Buchanan saw, both angry and apprehensive, if that was possible.

Under the cold black muzzle of his own pistol he crossed with deliberate unconcern to the stove, splashed scalding hot coffee from the pot into three tin cups and said, 'The Governor of Arizona himself'd have a hard time catching my ear before I've wet my whistle.' He turned from the stove, met the youngster's now bewildered gaze and placed two of the cups on the desk. 'One's yours, one's mine. This one's for the judge.' And leaving Josh Santee with a pistol and nothing to point it at, he swept the key ring from its hook and went through to the cells.

'My eyes are bad but my ears don't miss much,' Ed Payne said as Buchanan rattled the keys and opened the cell door. 'What's he hope to achieve, Tide?'

'A bed in the next cell is the first thing springs to mind,' Buchanan said grimly. 'But that won't solve a single damn thing, so let's see what else we can come up with.'

'We?' Ed Payne raised the hot cup to his lips with bony hands, his eyes bright and knowing.

'That's what I said.'

Back in the office, Buchanan found Josh Santee still standing stiffly in front of the desk. He was looking from the pistol to Buchanan, and the marshal got the impression that he was trying to figure out some way of escape without losing face.

Buchanan came to his rescue by fishing his lucifers out of his vest pocket and tossing them to the youngster.

'Light the lamp, Josh,' he said, and watched the boy look at the matches he had caught in his left hand, the six-gun he already held in his right, and realize that if he was going to strike a light he would have to put something down.

50

The six-gun ended up on the desk. Buchanan swept it away, eased the hammer. A match flared. There was the smell of warm coal oil, and lamplight flooded the office.

'Set,' Buchanan said as Santee turned away from the lamp. He slid the hot cup to the far side of the desk, watched the boy sit down, said quietly, 'So, what's all this about me leaving helpless citizens unprotected?' He sipped coffee, looked at the boy over the rim of the cup, raised an eyebrow. 'Who are they in danger from, son?'

'You damn well know who,' Santee said hotly.

'Well, in a roundabout way, yes, I do,' Buchanan said. 'But if you knew Wink Rachman was out of the Pen, wouldn't it be sensible to let me know, 'stead of ridin' into town when all those helpless citizens were in bed and lettin' loose with your pistol?'

'I....' The words died in Santee's throat. He grabbed the cup, managed to spill hot coffee on his pants as he took the cup to his lips, then burned his throat when he swallowed and finished up with tears in his eyes.

'Yeah,' Buchanan said, striving to keep his amusement from showing. 'I guess you figured your first duty was to Sally Grey – only she didn't see it that way.'

'Well....' Santee glared into his cup, then looked up at Buchanan. 'She did thank me,' he said, 'but that was after near drowning me with a jug of water she flang out'f her bedroom window.'

'Flang?' Buchanan said, now openly grinning. 'Josh, didn't you think that maybe she would have treated you with more respect if you'd already been wearing a badge?'

'I guess she would at that,' Santee said – then he did a swift double-take, traced backwards through the words he'd only half heard and looked at Buchanan open-mouthed.

'You ... what did you say, Marshal?'

'I said, if you'd already been wearing a badge she would have treated you with more respect.'

Santee's face was flushed. Then, feeling his way, he said, 'If I'd ... *already* ... been wearin' one, sort of suggests I wasn't wearin' one then but if I'd waited a while....'

'Well, ain't that what you walked in here for?' Buchanan asked innocently. 'Didn't you walk in to put your name forward for the vacant position of deputy marshal?'

Josh Santee took a slow, deep breath.

'Well, actually, no, I … that is, I … yes!'

The only time Buchanan had seen a man square his shoulders successfully while sitting was when he was in the saddle. Young Josh Santee managed it in the straight-backed office chair, with considerable poise. And the dark eyes that only moments ago had moved from apprehension to bewilderment were now shining with the prospect of the glory that would come to him when he pinned on a tarnished tin badge.

'Was that yes or no?' Buchanan asked.

'It was yes … sir,' Josh Santee said.

'Right,' Buchanan said, sliding open a desk drawer, taking out a glittering badge and heaving himself out of the chair all in one smooth movement.

'Come on, Deputy, let's go out back and get Judge Ed Payne to swear you in.'

FIVE

The light was failing.

In the Gila Desert, stretching for hundreds of square miles across the south-west corner of Arizona Territory, day turns to night almost as fast as a gunslinger can draw his six-shooter. But in that fast-waning light, still visible against the stretch of silver water, a lone steer lumbered up the banks of the Gila River. Maybe lumbered was the wrong word for what this steer was doing; *staggered* would be more appropriate, for this was no healthy animal soon to be rounded up and sold on the open market. This was a mighty sick beast, and so its slow, laboured progress from the muddy waters of the Gila to the cool shadows beneath the grey cottonwoods was in anything but a straight line. Several times, in a walk of no more than a hundred yards through cooling grass, its front legs buckled and it went down on its knees to remain there, head-hung, its open mouth trailing thin ropes of sticky saliva. Each time, strength returned. Each time, the steer regained its feet, and staggered onwards.

But at the edge of the cottonwoods it went down for the last time. Brush crackled under the heavy body. A dying breath was expelled like a moan of relief. A startled bird cried harshly. Wings flapped in the dusk.

In the sudden stillness, the silence was the silence of death. The steer's eyes, fast glazing, rolled, then settled to stare sightlessly at the faint outlines of a rising crescent moon.

From another, more easterly aspect, that crescent moon seemed to hang suspended in the branches of the cottonwoods, a beacon guiding the two riders who came splashing along the Gila's gravelly shallows in a fine spray of silvery water.

'Gone,' Vince Raper said.

'Maybe,' Matt Oakes said, 'you've been seein' things.'

'The hell I have!'

'Then if you saw it, we'll find it.'

Oakes's voice was placid, patient. Without laying it on too thick he had for some while been deliberately ribbing the dark, restless rider whose familiar monicker was Instant because that was the way he liked things to happen. There was no particular reason for the joshing; it was simply in Oakes's nature to act that way. If he thought about it at all he put it down to a way of passing the time, a habit he had acquired when serving his time riding drag, flank or point in the trail-driving days before Cole Santee had made him strawboss of the Tumbling S.

But while one part of his mind was working out ways of getting under his partner's thin skin, another part was ever watchful, and Oakes, too, had watched the steer emerge dripping from the Gila and begin its unsteady progress towards the trees.

And that was the difference between the two men. Raper had lost sight of the animal, and lost patience. Matt Oakes had also lost sight of it, but by swiftly quartering the dim, hazy landscape through eyes turned a little way away from where he was he was aiming to look, he had picked up movement. So now he rode some distance behind Vince Raper, content to let the man for whom things happened in a hurry – or not at all – work out for himself the only place the steer could have gone.

'Goddamn!' Raper called at last. 'Matt, there's only one damn place that blackjack steer can be at – and that's in those trees.'

Without waiting for a reply he kicked his mount out of the shallows and up the bank and set off across the open space at a fast gallop. By the time Oakes had followed and reached the edge of the timber at a more leisurely pace, Raper was out of the saddle and down on one knee where the under-brush had been broken and flattened by the still, bulky shape.

'Dead,' he said through his teeth. 'Matt, you got a light?'

Light flared as the strawboss scraped a match on the sole of his boot. Raper bent low, scrubbing the dead steer's hide with the flat of his gloved hand. His grunt of satisfaction had an ugly sound.

'Tumbling S,' he said, climbing to his feet. 'But someone's worked on it with a running iron.'

'Which makes it what, exactly?'

'Makes it nothing,' Raper said, 'and it don't need to. That's a Tumbling S steer, Matt, with its brand worked over – and the damn thing's lyin' on Silver Spur land!'

SIX

Inside Gila Bend's mercantile the oil lamps standing at either end of the counter cast long shadows, filling the room with the smell of hot coat oil to mingle with a host of other aromas that were like the breath of life to Tide Buchanan.

'Your pa ran a store, Tide,' Spencer Hill recalled, watching the marshal with some amusement as he stowed away the sack of Bull Durham he had just purchased, took a deep breath, and looked about him with obvious contentment.

'I was born on a pile of Navajo blankets in the corner of a room just like this,' Buchanan said, 'my ma shielded from pryin' eyes by another blanket draped over a rope. The first breath I took was laced with the smell of lye soap, the second with that from an open drum of axle grease pa was handin' to a mule-skinner – and, yeah, I guess that skinner was standin' inside a wide circle of his own ripe stink.'

Hill added a tin to a stack he was building,

said quietly, 'And in time you travelled the long, dusty, roundabout road from Utah to Arizona, on the way took four years off to fight a bloody war, ended up wearin' a badge, doin' a thankless job without help...'

'I got me a deputy,' Buchanan said. 'The judge just swore in young Josh Santee.'

'Jesus Christ in the foothills!'

'Spencer!'

Hill grabbed for the swaying stack of tins he had knocked with his elbow, smiled a hasty apology across the dim room to where Gayle Hill had glanced up from the haberdashery showcase to issue the sharp reprimand, then looked with genuine befuddlement at Tide Buchanan.

'With you likely to be called in to settle the dispute between Cole Santee and Silver Spur, ain't that puttin' the kid in an impossible situation? Placing him in direct confrontation with his own pa?'

'Sure, and Josh knows that. But he also knows Wink Rachman and his 'breed partner crossed the Gila at noon today, Spence. They were heading away from town, but Frank Parker reckons the only reason Rachman rode in six months ago was because he had his eyes on Harry Pepper's safe. Harry's of the same mind, and me, well, I don't reckon Wink'd break out of Yuma and drag a tough 'breed all the way across the Gila Desert just to settle a score with Sally Grey.'

Hill swore again, this time under his breath, absently tossed a tin from hand to hand. 'So, what have you got lined up against you, Tide? Tumbling S's likely to move on Silver Spur because Hank Carter had agreed a sale and Cole Santee won't listen to Beth. A couple of owlhoots out in the hills with their greedy eyes fixed on a pot of gold. A girl scared out of her wits.'

'And a judge locked up for … for what, exactly, Tide Buchanan?'

This was Gayle Hill talking. She had wandered across from her haberdashery display, and her level blue eyes were looking frankly at the marshal.

'For…' Buchanan smiled crookedly. 'For bein' a damn fool, Gayle, if you'll excuse my language. For doin' something he knew was wrong. For–'

'What Ed Payne did,' Gayle Hill said, interrupting with characteristic bluntness, 'may be morally wrong, but it's not something you expect to end up in jail for.'

'No.' Buchanan nodded agreement. 'No, it's not, Gay. But right now he's locked up all nice and cosy, and that's the way he'll stay until–'

'Until hell freezes over if I'm any judge,' Spencer Hill said with a broad grin. 'Only the hell I'm thinkin' of lives just across the street and it already well froze.'

'And that,' his wife said with a frown, 'is what your supper will be like, Mr Spencer Hill, if you don't curb your tongue.'

'Aw, c'mon, Gay!' Hill protested. He put his arm around his wife's shoulders, squeezed, saw the twitch of her soft lips as she suppressed a smile, and winked at Buchanan.

'So, what next, Marshal?'

'Well, when you were makin' your list of who's about to do what and when, you missed out one possible complication: Cole Santee's already made his move. Rode on the Spur around noon when, as far as I could make out, the two waddies Beth keeps on her books through the winter were out in the scrub doing a rough count of heads prior to round-up. Before I arrived on the scene the talk got heated and that short-trigger strawboss of Santee's managed to crease young Danny Carter's ribs with a .45 slug.'

'Oh, no!' Gayle said, somehow managing

61

an exclamation that was at once low and concerned, yet also an indignant cry of protest.

'Oh, the kid's not bad hurt,' Buchanan said, 'but if I know Danny he won't take this lying down. Trouble is, the situation between Spur and Tumbling S will lead him into something a sight more serious than a young kid taking pot shots at the stars.'

'Set tight,' Spencer Hill advised. 'See which of them warring factions out there jumps first.'

'I intend to,' Buchanan said, 'because right now I aim to get a bite to eat before my belly gets too familiar with my backbone.'

'You mean you're leaving that dangerous criminal you've got locked up in the care of a green youngster with a rusty pistol?' Gayle said sweetly.

'One thing that youngster never did,' Buchanan said, moving towards the door, 'was neglect that old Paterson his daddy gave him. Hell, I reckon that Paterson with its broken grip is about the most famous pistol in Gila Bend. Besides, if that cranky old prisoner does take inspiration from Wink Rachman and decide to bust out, well, as a sworn-in deputy Josh can lay his hands on two Winchester .44 carbines and a couple of shotguns – but my guess is the judge is already snoring loud enough to scare horses.'

He let the door click behind him, the heavy timber cutting off Spencer Hill's rich chuckle. The sun was down beyond the dark smudge of the Gila Mountains, the night closing in around Gila Bend to transform the town into an oasis of soft, scattered lights in the darkening desert landscape. Tide Buchanan took a deep breath of the cooling night air, glanced once across the street to where light spilled from the open door of his office, allowed himself a thin smile at the sight of a pair of booted legs crossed on the cluttered surface of his desk.

Then, after a day that had started with a pistol shot and ended with the same young kid who had done the shooting being sworn in and so doubling the number of lawmen working in Gila Bend, Tide Buchanan broadened his smile to one of considerable satisfaction and set about attending to his personal needs.

During his spell as Marshal of Gila Bend – which now stretched back some five years – Buchanan had learned that leaving irritating problems to soak at the back of his mind for a spell often saw at least some of the answers come bubbling to the surface. And so it was with his current troubles.

After leaving the mercantile he enjoyed a hot bath, went to his room in Gila Bend's only hotel to change his clothes, then ate well at the same establishment's dining room. From there he simply stepped out onto the plankwalk, belched comfortably, crossed the street into the evening bustle of McMahon's saloon and, almost inevitably, found himself sharing a table with Frank Parker.

The old hostler's apple-brown face was rarely raised far from his glass, but he was clear-eyed, and between mouthfuls of beer he spoke with the authority and wisdom of a man who had once tracked Indians for the army and in more recent years had watched a whole world go by from the gaping doors of his livery barn. Always interesting, he eventually worked his way around to a subject that grabbed Buchanan by the throat and begged his attention.

'Maybe a year ago,' Parker was saying, 'I was standin' up against the bar sort of listenin' with one ear to Cole Santee and Hank Carter dickering over the price of Silver Spur.'

He paused to gulp a mouthful of warm beer, grimaced, squinted across the table at Buchanan.

'Bear in mind,' the old hostler said, 'at that time of night I was standin' with difficulty and the help of both my elbows while tryin' to hold this crazy room still with the hand that wasn't already hangin' on to my drink.'

'This,' Buchanan said, 'must've been close to midnight, nearing the end of a drinking session that started when the last rider collected his horse.'

'And,' Parker said, grinning happily at the memory, 'it had been an unusually quiet day.'

'Nevertheless,' Buchanan prompted.

'I'm a respectable businessman – as you know – and apart from gathering choice bits of gossip to regurgitate....' This word seemed to tickle the old man, and for long seconds he drooped weakly over the beer glass that was held in both hands beneath his fleshy nose, chuckling like a flooded creek.

'To regurgitate,' he finally managed, wet-eyed, 'when the time was ripe. Anyhow, apart from doin' that, I was mindin' my own business – which, at that time, was the serious attempt to find out how much beer a man needed to pour down his throat before he'd float out the door.'

'Get on with it, Frank!'

'Chug Austin, on the other hand,' Parker said, his blue eyes now hard and bright, 'never could pass himself off as a gentleman.'

'Austin!' Tide Buchanan breathed.

'Him and that goddamn filthy red bandanna around his greasy grey hair and his long Injun moccasins, and that rifle that'd blow a hole clear through the Gila Mountains – hell, he was prancin' around splashin' rot-gut whiskey in the sawdust and collidin' with the tables so that the poker players were grabbin' for their cards and their drinks…. Anyhow, after a while Cole Santee and Hank Carter lost patience, grabbed a hold of an arm and a leg apiece and heaved old Chug out into the street.'

'I know Austin, vaguely recall hearing something about that fracas from Spence,' Buchanan said, 'but if I remember right, I was out of town at the time.'

'Business, or pleasure?' Parker said, his eyes innocent.

'The question I asked,' Tide Buchanan said, 'was if two fellers came out of the Gila Desert and crossed the river in a mostly east to west direction – where would they likely be headed?'

'An' I just told you,' Frank Parker said. 'You know as well as I do Chug Austin hangs out in them hills, slips down into Buckeye or Palo Verde when he needs supplies he can't shoot or drag out the river.'

'A place like that,' Buchanan said thoughtfully, 'would serve any number of useful purposes for a couple of galoots on the run from the law.'

'Damn right it would,' Parker said. 'You said they was headin' in that direction, and if there's anyone in these parts can be depended on to go directly against the dictates of law and order – for the sheer hell of it – that's Chug Austin.'

Buchanan ran a hand over hair that was still damp from his bath, then reached for his beer.

'What troubles me is, Austin's cabin is too damn far out to make any sense if their sole aims is to rob the bank.'

'But mighty handy if Rachman's got Harry Pepper's bank at the back of his mind – held in reserve, so to speak – but his sights set firm on acquirin' Silver Spur for his own purposes.'

'Which raises another thorny question,' Tide Buchanan said. 'What the hell good reason would a man like Wink Rachman have for takin' over a working ranch?'

'Cover?'

'Yeah, exactly what I was thinkin',' Buchanan agreed. 'Could be he's plannin' on assemblin' a crew of tough gents, and usin' them to relieve Cole Santee of prime cattle.'

The marshal was still musing over that possibility when the saloon's swing doors slapped back and the chunky figure of Spencer Hill came in out of the darkening night and headed for the bar. At the same time, from across the room where a battered piano was gathering dust on a low wooden platform, a shapely girl in a low-cut dress drifted towards Buchanan's table. Her heavily painted lips were parted, her dark eyes moody.

'How long are you keepin' the judge locked up, Marshal?'

'For as long as it takes, Belle.'

A frown creased her powdered brow. 'What exactly does that mean?'

'I'm not too sure myself, never having been in this situation.'

'It's him that's in a situation,' she said,

68

'and it's you that's keepin' him there.'

'Yeah,' Buchanan said, 'but he's only got himself to blame – and another I could mention who ain't too far from this table.'

The girl flushed. 'What if I said from now on I'd–'

'There's nothing you can say that would help,' Buchanan cut in. 'You were involved, but you're not the reason I put him in jail.'

'So maybe you should go chase the reason, and not pick on the judge,' the girl said, and with a toss of her head she turned and walked away.

'*Tooshay,*' Frank Parker said softly, and Tide Buchanan allowed himself a somewhat sheepish grin.

By this time, Spencer Hill had ordered his drink, caught sight of Buchanan and Parker, added two more glasses to the one he was carrying and come over to their table in a rush to slop copious quantities of beer as he almost fell into a chair.

'If it was closer to midnight,' Frank Parker said, straight-faced, 'I'd be fired up enough to take exception to having beer splashed on my best shirt.'

'If it was any closer to midnight,' Hill responded, also deadpan, 'you'd have that shirt off your back and be wringin' it out

69

over your open mouth.'

'You did say *best* shirt?' Buchanan said, winking at the owner of the mercantile.

Parker grinned as he pushed his empty glass to one side and reached for the full one. 'Best shirt, only shirt....' He shrugged, raised his glass to Spencer Hill, continued the movement all the way to his mouth and began to lower the level of the beer.

'On the way over,' Hill said, 'I talked to the town's new deputy.'

Frank Parker almost choked on his beer, blinked, stared owlishly at Hill.

'You mean to tell me this feller's finally seen sense, got hisself a helper that lets you off the hook?'

'I wouldn't exactly call it seein' sense,' Hill drawled, 'and nor will you when you hear the deputy's name.'

'So, what did Josh have to say?' Buchanan said.

'Goddamn!' Frank Parker breathed, eyes wide. 'You got Josh Santee, pinnin' on a badge and goin' up against his pa?'

'And doin' it right well,' Hill said. 'Tide, we chatted a spell, and during the course of it Josh mentioned that his pa's been losing stock. Just a trickle, no more than a few head, but it's been happenin' every month.'

Parker looked amazed. 'Gettin' hit by rustlers before Wink Rachman arrived back?'

'Frank, will you for Christ's sake let Spence finish!' Buchanan glared at the old hostler, then said to Hill, 'Santee's made no complaints to me.'

Hill shrugged. 'You know Cole. Makes his own laws, backs them with hired guns.'

'Of itself, his losing stock don't affect the situation we discussed earlier – unless there's more to it.'

'According to Josh, his pa's pointing the finger at Beth Carter.'

'Come on!' Buchanan scoffed. 'She's got Danny, those riders I told you about she kept on through the winter, out on the range doing a rough head count....' He paused, lips pursed, eyes narrowed. 'In any case, how the hell does Santee know what's goin' missing? Spring round-ups ain't started. All his cattle are spread far and wide, wanderin' the scrub.'

'His riders are out, too, Tide. And they've found Tumbling S steers with doctored brands.'

'He says!'

Hill shook his head. 'No. Josh says. He was ridin' with them. It was him found two dead steers, in a dry wash.'

'How doctored?' Buchanan was frowning.

'Runnin' iron. Tumblin' S burned out, altered to look like a crude spur.'

'Still could be a set up,' Frank Parker said, wiping froth from his lips. 'Wouldn't be the first time a rancher altered his own brands to incriminate an innocent neighbour.'

Spencer Hill was watching Buchanan. 'Something, Tide?'

'Rustling was mentioned by Santee when I was out at Spur. At the time, I thought it was rage driving him to wild talk. But maybe he has lost stock. Or maybe what he said was for my benefit. Maybe...' – he shook his head – 'maybe Beth Carter is hiding something – and for sure, young Danny got trigger-happy when Tumbling S riders appeared in Spur's yard.'

'But the altered brands are fact, Tide, and a mighty powerful weapon. If Santee moves fast he can drive Beth Carter off Silver Spur and, with him holdin' those hides as evidence, every cattleman in south-west Arizona'll wag his head in approval.'

Buchanan took a deep breath, let it out slowly. 'And here was me,' he said, 'hopin' for an early night.'

'You want me along for the ride?'

'I'm not anticipating trouble, Spence. But I need to ask Beth some questions, get her side of the story.'

'Won't talk wait until morning?'

Buchanan scraped back from the table. 'What was it you said? If Santee moves fast he can drive Beth off Spur? That sounds to me like time ain't on Beth's side, and if I'm to put a stop to what Cole Santee appears to be threatening, I need hard facts – and I need them now.'

SEVEN

'I think you should ride to the line cabin, fetch Bill and Eddy,' Beth Carter said quietly.

'Ma, you've got me, and that old Remington scattergun. Santee tries anything, we'll give as good as we get.'

The big room was still warm from the long day's hot sun, the heat of which had been soaked up and retained by the massive log walls, and the smell of gun-oil was thick and heady under pungent wood smoke and the aroma of fine cooking. Danny Carter, ribs heavily bandaged, was working on his sixgun with an oily rag. Beth was watching him tensely from her seat by the fire, aware that he was doing his best to help and encourage her but knowing, deep down, that no matter what the boy did it would not be enough.

At sundown she had heard riders, had ordered Danny to stay in the house and had taken her shotgun to the edge of the cottonwoods and watched apprehensively

74

from deep cover as Matt Oakes and Vince Raper rode in from Gila. They had dismounted with a jingle of bridles, gone into a huddle. The murmur of their voices had drifted to her through the gloom. She had detected anger, and had pressed back fearfully into the shadows as the rising moon glinted on the bright metal of the Tumbling S riders' weapons.

Then they had ridden away, using spurs cruelly and taking the fast, easy route to the Tumbling S along the banks of the Gila, and after a while Beth had ventured from her hiding place, cocked the shotgun, and walked down to where the two men had lingered. Her mind had felt numb as she stared down at what they had found.

'Who's doing it, Danny?' she said now. 'That's the third steer in as many weeks, and this time Matt Oakes found it. But how? He didn't ride all this way by chance.'

'Santee's doin' it,' Danny said tightly. 'Nobody's stealin' his stock. But he needs an excuse to move us on, so he's planting Tumbling S steers with doctored brands on Spur land.'

'That doesn't ring true.' Beth was frowning, her eyes troubled. 'Everything Cole Santee has done has been within the law.

Your father agreed to sell Spur. Santee is now pushing me hard to honour that agreement. But he is not a devious man, Danny. Hard enough so that I can see him using physical force to drive us off Spur, yes – but he's not the kind of man who would need a manufactured excuse.'

'Then what?' Danny asked hotly. He snapped the cylinder back into his six-gun, said, 'If we aint alterin' brands, who–'

And then he broke off.

Beth Carter's haunted eyes met and drowned in the dark pools of the boy's fear. For long seconds they listened, mother and son, scarcely breathing.

'Riders,' Danny said. His voice was tight, his face pale and glistening under its tan.

'Tide said we would talk, maybe he's come back....'

She looked wide-eyed at her injured son, hearing the fierce rattle of approaching hooves, knowing that several riders were bearing down on Silver Spur and that she was desperately clutching at fragile straws because they were, surely, from Tumbling S.

Then, tightening her lips, she came up out of the chair in a swift and desperate lunge to reach for the shotgun.

But it was too late.

The first shot took out the window so that a shower of jagged shards exploded into the room. The overwhelming noise and the sharp crack of the second shot drowned Beth's cry of fear and pitched the room into darkness as it shattered the oil lamp and sent flames licking across the table. That inky darkness that might have given the Carters time to slip away through the house to the back door lasted scant seconds. The pool of spilled coal-oil spread across the table. Black smoke billowed ahead of the spreading flames. And, closely following that second shot, a blazing firebrand came spinning through the shattered window. It splattered its own share of burning coal-oil on curtains that flapped wildly in the wind of its passing. As the thin blue cotton ignited and swiftly flared in the draught, the crude torch fashioned from a broken fence-post and soaked, knotted rags whirled end-over-end across the room leaving a trail of smoke and flame. It thudded against the far wall. Blazing coal-oil splashed on logs that were devoid of moisture but sticky with resin. In that instant the wall was transformed into a wall of yellow fire, its blistering heat forcing Beth and Danny to protect the seared skin of their faces with upflung arms and driving them back towards the front door.

The door was flung open to crash back against the wall.

'Outside, fast!' a voice called, soft, but stamped with a terrible urgency.

Danny Carter was still holding his six-gun.

He swivelled on booted heel and toe, flipped up the Colt, snapped back the hammer. But the room was rapidly becoming smoke-filled. His wide eyes were red and streaming. Even as he levelled the pistol, a racking cough tore through his frame, ripping at the recent bullet-wound. A cry of agony escaped from between tight lips, clenched teeth. The six-gun drooped, wavered.

In that instant the man in the doorway sprang. He was masked, the bandanna pulled up across his face concealing all but his glittering black eyes. A carbine was held in both hands. His bound carried him like a pouncing lion through the swirling smoke. As he sprang he swung the carbine sideways, putting hard muscle into the blow. The butt cracked against the side of Danny Carter's head. His eyes rolled. Without a sound he crashed to the floor.

'You swine, Vince Raper!' Beth screamed.

As she leaped to her son's aid, hands fluttering, the dark man callously swept her aside. The bony thrust of his elbow sank deep into soft, womanly curves. She gasped with pain. Knocked off balance, she stumbled towards the open door. The gunman took the carbine in his left hand, reached down with his right to grasp Danny Carter's collar. With a grunt, he braced his legs and began dragging the boy across the floor.

To Beth, doubled over with pain, breath rasping in her throat, eyes blurred with tears, the scene was a scene from hell. The living-room of her home was an inferno, the fierce heat unbearable, flames crackling and spitting, leaping and licking, black smoke swirling high, the light at once dazzling yet dim as first the thick smoke and then the madly dancing flames gained the ascendency.

Through that nightmare vision the dark masked man with the cruel eyes and glittering carbine dragged the body of her son, the bright red blood from the boy's fresh head wound like a glistening snail-trail across the floor.

There was nothing Beth could do but turn away.

The open doorway offered succour, salvation. She stumbled through it blindly, sucking in deep gulps of cool, clean air. The night caught at her throat. She coughed, lifted her head, dashed the tears from her eyes and saw the two skittish horses backing nervously from the flames, the two implacable, malevolent riders with their impressive bulk and the deadly menace of their drawn weapons.

And she saw, alongside them, two riderless saddled horses she recognized, and she was appalled to realize that before they had driven her from her home, the Tumbling S men had come stealthily in out of the night to invade her corral and barn and saddle the horses that would take her and Danny....

Take them where?

'I should hang him,' Cole Santee said, chest swelling as he sat tall in the saddle, lifting his deep voice to be heard above the crackling of the flames. 'They hang rustlers, and your boy has been party to rustling.'

'You're lying,' Beth said, and the injustice of the man's accusation caused her voice to break in a sob of bitter frustration.

"The proof's there,' Vince Raper snarled, gesturing towards the cottonwoods.

He jerked viciously at Danny's collar, let

him thump heavily down the three wide steps, dragged him part way to the saddled horses then dropped him in the dirt like a limp sack of grain. When he turned and ripped off the bandanna, the hungry flames that had broken through the dry shingle roof of the house with a fierce roar lit up the Tumbling S rider's unshaven, saturnine countenance, and Beth knew the mask had been worn to protect him from the smoke, not from her gaze.

These men saw no reason to hide their faces. The running-iron brand she had seen on the dead steer they had discovered in the cottonwoods justified the direst retribution. Cole Santee had baldly stated the awful truth. Evidence of rustling had been found on Silver Spur land. On that justification these men could hang her boy from the nearest tree, cut down the body and take it belly-down over his horse into Gila Bend to dump it on the steps of Tide Buchanan's jailhouse.

'Matt,' Santee said, 'help Vince get him on his horse.'

The strawboss swung down. His dragoon moustache was yellow in the flickering light, his eyes chips of cold stone. Together, he and the dark gunman heaved Danny Carter across his saddled horse, let him hang there, belly down, legs and arms dangling.

'I don't care where, or how,' Santee said, 'but I want you off this land. Silver Spur is mine. You had your chance to sell, but turned it down. So be it. Hank Carter was not a good man, but neither was he a thief. You were robbing me, and for you to accept my offer would in any case have been adding insult to injury. I know that now, know also what you and your boy were doing – and I've acted accordingly.'

It was a long speech for a taciturn man. Every word of it, from where Santee sat, was the truth. He pinned Beth Carter with his cold, ruthless gaze for several long seconds, watched her pitilessly until she deliberately broke the spell by averting her eyes and moved away from the blazing house to cross the yard and drop to her knees alongside her son.

Then, with a barked command, Cole Santee wheeled his horse and led his strawboss and hired gun away from Silver Spur at a furious gallop. A yellow dust cloud swirled in their wake, drifting and settling in the flickering light. The receding hoofbeats faded from a roll of thunder to a distant whisper. And in a heavy silence weighted by heat of the blaze and broken only by the crackle of burning timber, Beth Carter bowed her head and wept hot tears as Danny Carter groaned through his teeth, opened his eyes and struggled to rise.

In the flat desert landscape the glow from the burning ranch house lighting the night sky was visible from many miles away, a lurid, shimmering canopy in sharp contrast to the cold light of the moon.

At the sight of it, Tide Buchanan's jaw set. The blue roan was well fed and rested, and willingly answered the light touch of the marshal's spurs, his sudden urgent call for more speed. The big horse stretched out eagerly, began eating up the miles with a tireless, loping stride, and all the while the glow overhead was a torment to Buchanan. But it was a fading torment, a torment that perceptibly lost strength and colour, its ominous presence waning with every mile that passed beneath the roan's flying hooves until, as the silver ribbon of the Gila became visible over the flats, the fiery glow was at last overpowered by the brilliance of the high, moonlit white clouds.

For the second time in the space of twelve hours, Tide Buchanan hammered into the yard at Silver Spur. But this time there was no trio of aggressive horsemen to greet him with their menacing presence, no fretting, bloodstained youth wilting on the gallery, no feisty young woman looking along the barrel of a shotgun.

The house built by Hank Carter was a flat expanse of blackened, smouldering embers at whose heart the glow of the recent fire still angrily pulsed. And as he gazed upon the ruins, hope sank in the breast of Gila Bend's marshal, and a coldness crept over him that was composed of fear, and a sudden, deadly purpose.

He dismounted swiftly, left the roan to wander with trailing reins and crossed to the steps which had, miraculously, escaped the flames. But they led nowhere, and Buchanan touched them lightly with his boot then skirted the forlorn planks of wood and edged close to what had once been the ranch house's front wall.

Here, the heat was intense, searing through the thin soles of his boots, devouring the very air he breathed. He lifted a gloved hand to shield his face, gasping open-mouthed as he squinted sideways through narrowed eyes into the living, crimson heart of the embers. But there was nothing to see. If a woman and a boy had died in the blaze there was no tangible evidence: if they had escaped....

He turned away from the glow, sickened, was met by an after image that made the blackness appear to close in like a wall all around him. In a few moments he could see clearly again, but he was no skilled tracker, and after a brief glance at the churned dust of the yard he whistled the roan, swung into the saddle. And, knowing that the voice inside him that screamed for action was the voice of panic, there, alongside the ruins of Beth Carter's home, Tide Buchanan deliberately took time to roll and light a cigarette.

Was he gazing at the handiwork of Beth's outlaw brother, Wink Rachman? Or was this the doing of the powerful Cole Santee, a man who near as dammit owned Silver Spur but had seen the prize plucked from his grasp when a strong, single-minded widow took over the reins?

If Santee, had the Tumbling S boss razed Silver Spur to the ground without warning, or mercy – or had he relented sufficiently to allow its two occupants to escape? Knowing the burly rancher, Buchanan would have bet a year's wages on the latter, and with the cigarette drooping from his lips he rode out of the yard and walked the roan the short distance to the cottonwoods.

By now the high clouds had thickened, veiling the face of the moon. The light was thin, shadows deep, Buchanan's sweep along the woods bordering the Gila no more than a token search. If Beth and Danny were there, they would see him; if they chose to ignore him, they would have no difficulty staying hidden until daylight.

One thing was for sure: if he wanted the truth about the recent incidents at Silver Spur, one man would have the answer.

The direction of Buchanan's search had carried him west along the cottonwoods. On the banks of the Gila River he flicked away the cigarette, watched it arc away, sparking, thought he heard the soft hiss as it hit the water but knew that was the workings of imagination sharpened by fancied horrors.

Then, with a last, grim glance back at the smouldering ruins that had once been Silver Spur, Buchanan lifted the roan's head and turned it towards Cole Santee's Tumbling S.

EIGHT

'Maybe now,' Wink Rachman said, 'you'll thank me for bustin' out of the Pen and comin' back to you.'

The cabin was cluttered and smoke-filled, a stinking hell-hole of a shack built and lived in by a man who washed if he accidentally fell in a creek, changed his clothes when they wore out. A glowing, black iron stove belched wood smoke from a split flue. Greasy tin plates containing scraps of blackened potato and half-chewed meat littered the table by a small, glassless window across which was nailed old, torn sacking. Tin cans, kindling, ashes, mud-caked boots, mouldy scraps of food and sundry items of worn or broken equipment were scattered over the dirt floor, and the oil lamp hanging from an iron hook embedded in the sod roof smoked as badly as the stove and provided about as much dim light as that hot metal through a chimney blackened with oily soot.

Pedro Torres was sitting at the table, his

black eyes glittering as he angrily smoked a thin black cheroot. Danny Carter was at the back of the room, lost in deep shadows, lying on an iron cot covered with filthy animal skins with his eyes closed and a wet cloth draped over his forehead. Beth Carter was sitting on the end of the same bed, her face pale. And in a chair draped in an old cow-hide close to that crackling, belching stove reclined Chug Austin, lank grey hair held back from his grimy face by a sweat-stained red headband, bloodshot grey eyes watchful and amused, skinny, moccasined legs stretched out as he puffed at an evil smelling pipe that gurgled wetly.

'And I suppose I should also thank you for murdering Hank?' Beth said now, and across the table from the glowering Torres, Wink Rachman laughed.

'You and me, we'll make a team,' he said, 'in every way. Put Cole Santee in his place. Relieve Harry Pepper of surplus cash that's cluttering up his safe. Move on to fresh pastures, start a life together.'

'All right,' Beth said bleakly, 'I admit I need your help. But that's as far as it goes, Charlie. No bank job. No move.'

'Why do we need help from an owlhoot on the run?' Danny Carter said faintly, eyes still shut. 'We need help, go see Tide Buchanan, Ma. Him and Spence Hill, Judge Payne, they're the people'll sort out Santee.'

'It's not that simple,' Beth said. 'Done like that, we'd need to wait for the law to decide one way or another – and although we know we've done nothing wrong, on the evidence Santee has, we could lose.'

Torres, the 'breed, swore softly, mashed the cheroot on one of the greasy plates. 'Yeah,' he drawled, glaring at Rachman, 'but I rode across the desert to rob a bank, not fight someone else's range war. Now we get here, you talk about a woman being part of the team. Listen. I tell you now, I don't ride alongside no woman.'

The drooping left eyelid that had earned Charlie Rachman his sobriquet flickered. He said softly, savagely, 'There'll be no war. Cole Santee's all bluster. He'll back down.'

'You just ain't listenin', are you, boy?'

Beth looked quickly at the old man in the creaking wooden chair by the stove. He had taken the wet pipe from his mouth for the first time since Rachman and Torres had brought her and Danny up from the burning shell of Silver Spur, mentally and physically exhausted, almost two hours ago. An hour earlier, the two escaped convicts had ridden into the Silver Spur yard as she had known they would as soon as Cole Santee blurted out the news of the jail break. The fact that they had done so by the light of the dying flames when she and Danny were sitting in the saddle dazed and bewildered was opportune, though not what Beth would have wanted, given a choice.

This filthy old reprobate, she realized, had soaked up the heat of the stove and sucked at his stinking pipe and come to the same conclusion she had reached: that Charlie Rachman, never the most stable of men, was drifting into a land of fantasy and talking a load of contradictory nonsense. Now, emphasizing each point with a stab of his pipe, Austin went on to elaborate.

'In the first place, Cole Santee ain't likely to back off. Silver Spur's been stealin' his cattle. He's got doctored hides as evidence, and in all he's done so far he's got the unwritten code of the West on his side.'

'But he's lying through his teeth,' Danny Carter said.

'Maybe, maybe not. But what ain't in any doubt is, he's holdin' proof of theft.'

'All he's got is proof that *somebody* was stealing his cattle,' Beth said.

Austin grinned. 'Ain't nobody else *could've*

done it.' His grey eyes flashed a challenge, then he turned again to Rachman. 'But in the second place supposin', just supposin', you best Cole Santee. What then? Silver Spur's back with its rightful owner, and she just told you that's it, finished. No bank robbery. No move to them pastures new. Hell, that happens you've just got her back her *old* pastures.'

'Leave her,' Pedro Torres said flatly. 'Ride on.'

'No.' There was the sheen of sweat on Rachman's brow.

'So what the hell do you want? If, for her sake, for some stupid sentimental reason, you go against this man Santee and he refuses to back off, you kill him – so then what? With a posse out hunting for you, you think you have still got a chance of riding into Gila Bend, of robbing the bank?'

'I don't know!' Rachman's fist slammed down on the table, rattling the plates. He pushed his chair back, sent it clattering to the floor, swivelled to kick out wildly and sent a tin can clanging against the stove.

'But I sure do,' Pedro Torres said, unimpressed. 'You spoke about it often enough in Yuma. You want this woman. And because she knows it, she's got you jumping through hoops like a goddamn trained dog. And all for nothing.'

'Because when she's got what she wants,' Chug Austin said, spitting wetly into the ashes at his feet, 'you think she'll have any time for you?'

'Maybe,' Charlie 'Wink' Rachman said, his eyes glaring balefully through the thick haze of that stifling hot room at Beth Carter, 'maybe when the time comes, she'll have no goddamn option.'

'Jesus!' Chug Austin shook his head in disgust. 'I must be crazy myself,' he said, 'to give house room to a madman.'

A dog began yapping as Tide Buchanan rode past the big corrals in which the young geldings rough-broken for the spring round-ups by Wes Lake stood dozing in the thin moonlight, skirted the buckboard he had last seen being swung away from the mercantile by the wrangler, and headed for the Tumbling S ranch house. The dog's warning of a stranger's approach was picked up on the faint breeze and a horse whinnied in the barn, another answered from a distance. At the same time the bunkhouse door creaked open and warm lamplight cast a man's shadow long across the yard.

Then Buchanan was at the tie-rail in front of the house's long, wide gallery, and as he swung down and looped the reins over the pole, the front door opened and the massive figure of Cole Santee stomped out onto the scrubbed boards, shirt sleeves rolled back from massive forearms thick with wiry black hair, huge dark head bare.

'All right, Matt,' he called, 'I'll handle this,' and across the yard somebody said something Buchanan didn't catch and the bunkhouse door slammed.

'Come on in,' Santee said gruffly. 'There ain't no point askin' what this visit is about, so we might as well get to it.'

The big room was pleasantly warm, the dark polished furniture of the high quality one would expect to find in the home of a man who had made his money from cattle and invested wisely. Buchanan tossed his dusty hat onto a glossy leather chair, stood awkwardly while Santee poured drinks in two crystal glasses, then accepted his with a grunt of thanks and sat down.

The big rancher remained standing. In the muted glow from the single lamp his glass flashed glittering highlights, and both his swarthiness and his bulk were emphasized: he was big in size, big in influence; among his business colleagues in Gila Bend he could count on the support of Judge Ed Payne, and although Tide Buchanan also numbered the judge among his friends he sensed that nothing worthwhile could come of this visit.

'You want to know, I used coal-oil to burn them out because they were stealing my cattle,' Cole Santee said. Acting totally in character, he had bluntly stated his case. Now, he sipped the fine whiskey and waited without concern for the marshal's response.

'One question,' Buchanan said. 'Were the Carters in the house when your men put it to the torch?'

'That would have been foolish in the extreme,' Santee said, and Buchanan noted that cynical reply. Not cruel, not wicked, but foolish; such a barbaric act – well within the man's capabilities – had been dismissed as impracticable only because, in the long term, it would have harmed Cole Santee's reputation and his bank balance.

'We let off a few pistol shots, gave them a scare,' Santee said, 'then brought up their saddled horses so they could ride out.' He shrugged. 'I'm surprised you didn't pass them on your way here.'

'You think they'll have ridden to town?'

'Where else? Beth Carter's friendly with that seamstress, Sally Grey. She's got more rooms than she needs. I'd expect them to stay there, at least for a while.'

'There ain't too many men packing badges in this part of the West,' Buchanan said, choosing his words, feeling his way. 'I'm one of them, you know it, and it ain't all that much of a ride to Gila Bend. So I reckon to take the law into your own hands you've got hard evidence a crime, or crimes, have been committed – or you've got evidence, but you moved fast because you know damn well it wouldn't stand up in court.'

Santee chuckled. 'The problem with courts,' he said, 'is they put good evidence on display and some fancy lawyer comes along and tears it to shreds.' His face sobered. 'How many times have you seen a man who's guilty as hell walk free, Marshal?'

'Rather that,' Buchanan said, 'than an innocent man with his neck stretched, swinging from a tree.' He smiled wryly, again thinking of this man's abiding concern for his own reputation. 'But I guess you had that in mind when you stopped short of a hangin'.' He watched as the rancher walked across to the window, gazed out into the darkness, said softly, 'Another question, Santee: can you give me one good reason why Beth Carter would even consider stealing your cattle?'

Cole Santee turned. The glass was forgotten in his hand, his eyes hooded, his lips thrust forward. He seemed to be giving lengthy thought to Buchanan's question, which Buchanan knew was a tricky one. Evidence of theft was damning, but even a thief needs a motive. If Beth Carter had no reason to steal, then Cole Santee's violent reaction had been precipitate. He would have been wiser to hold back and look elsewhere for his rustlers, and the fact that he had not done so put a huge question mark against his own motives. Retribution, or land-grabbing? The urge to see justice meted out, or a lust for property that led him to use the loss of a few steers as justification for theft of a different kind?

Santee stirred, shook his head as if his deliberations were a waste of time, then tossed back the last of the whiskey with a jerk of his thick wrist.

'My boy say when he's comin' home?'

'He could've come instead of me,' Buchanan said, and saw the rancher frown. 'Then

96

it would've been him askin' the questions, and not gettin' answers.'

'What the hell's that supposed to mean?'

'It means I asked a question you chose to ignore – and that your boy Josh is wearin' a deputy's badge.'

Santee jerked as if struck. Then his jaw muscles bunched. 'We'll see about that.'

'All done legal,' Buchanan said. 'Sworn in by your friend, Ed Payne.'

Santee's smile left his eyes cold and hard. 'The old man you've turned into a jailbird.'

'Aw, hell,' Buchanan said in mock protest, 'we all know what that's about, Santee.' He came out of his chair, reached for his hat and planted it, hitched his gunbelt and said, 'Give it a few days. Before you know it Ed'll be in his office with his specs perched on the end of his nose. He'll be back in his old routine, the job he does better than any man I know – puttin' the fear of God into every law breaker in the territory.'

He tipped his hat, made for the door and, as a parting shot tossed into the silence, said, 'You might bear that in mind, Santee, before you move onto Silver Spur land and start treatin' it as your own.'

NINE

At ten o'clock that morning Tide Buchanan finally thumped noisily into his stuffy office, found it deserted, walked through to the cell block and discovered Deputy Town Marshal Josh Santee and Judge Ed Payne jawing away like old friends through the bars of the judge's strap-steel cage.

In the relatively short time since leaving the Tumbling S, Buchanan had packed in the tedious return ride to Gila Bend, snatched a couple of hours' solid sleep, endured a bracing strip wash in ice-cold water and enjoyed the walk over to the livery barn where, after a single question, he had put a proposition to Frank Parker that brought a joyous glint to the old man's eyes.

On the short walk from there to the jailhouse he had thought briefly of rapping on the heavy door of the judge's office and doing some hard talking to Agnes Payne, neé, Smallbone – but after one swift glance at the angle of the sun he had, with considerable relief, used the earliness of the hour as an excuse for hurrying on by.

He had spoken once after leaving Parker: to the pert and blushing young seamstress, Sally Grey, who had passed him on her way from Spencer Hill's mercantile with a basket of provisions, her eyes demurely lowered. He had asked her the same question, and received the same answer: no, Beth and Danny Carter had not been seen in Gila Bend, and they most certainly were not staying with her.

The young woman's uncharacteristic blush at the encounter had been noted without comment by Buchanan, who guessed, with a feeling of pleasant warmth that was most welcome after the bleakness of the past hours, that the girl had made her peace with the boy who had broken her sleep with a pistol shot and suffered a soaking for his pains.

And so the first question to his new deputy – in what Buchanan acknowledged with inner amusement to be a spell of official probing bordering on rudeness – was on that very subject.

The result was another rush of blood, this time to the dark, unshaven countenance of young Josh Santee, who mumbled something about the confounded fickleness of all females and rushed off unbidden to make coffee.

'That smoke I smell?' Ed Payne said shrewdly.

'On me?' Buchanan nodded. 'I guess it clings. Silver Spur was burned to the ground last night. Cole Santee's doing. He admits it, shows no damned remorse.'

'Why should he? It's what he's been working up to.' The judge studied Buchanan as tin pots clattered in the other room. 'How's Beth taking it?'

'Cole Santee allowed her and Danny saddled horses, let them ride. He was under the impression they'd head for town.'

'And?'

'Not so. If they were here, Frank Parker would have seen them.'

'Ain't that a fact!'

'So,' Buchanan said, 'I've enlisted the help of the best damn tracker in the territory—'

'Which wouldn't, by some strange chance, be that same Frank Parker?'

'—and as soon as I've briefed my deputy I'll be on my way.'

The outer office door was kicked open and Josh Santee came through carrying three steaming tin cups. When each man had taken the first, bracing sip of the bitter black brew, the boy looked inquisitively at Buchanan.

'Voices carry,' he said by way of explanation. 'I guess you'll be headin' back to Silver Spur, see if Frank can pick up the trail.'

'You guess right,' Buchanan said. 'You reckon you can cope for a while longer?'

'Don't see why not – unless the judge is plannin' a jail break.'

'Oh, there's all manner of fiendish initiation tests us wily convicts dream up for young deputies still wet behind the ears,' Ed Payne said in sepuchral tones. He winked at Buchanan, then frowned and flicked his eyes towards the half-open door as a deep voice with a peculiar, indescribable intonation, called through from the office.

When Tide Buchanan strode through to investigate – a precautionary hand on his pistol – it was to find a man slumped weakly in the chair on the far side of the desk. He was lean and hatless and caked with trail dust. His black hair was damp with sweat, his blue eyes sunken, his face unshaven and gaunt with a terrible suffering. The front of his shirt was soaked with congealed blood. Before it had congealed that blood had flowed freely, so that the star with a tiny ball on each of its six points, pinned to the front of that ruined shirt, now gave the illusion of being fashioned from old, rusted metal.

But, though caked with dried blood, it was still recognizable as the badge of a US Marshal.

Behind Tide Buchanan, a young Josh Santee said wonderingly, 'That there's Johnny Vaughan, Marshal, the man rode after Wink Rachman.'

'There's things you need to know about Rachman,' Johnny Vaughan said.

The US Marshal's face was tight with pain. He was stripped to the waist, lying awkwardly propped up on a table. Gila Bend's sawbones, a thin, angry-looking man with strands of dark hair plastered across a mottled scalp, was probing with metal forceps held in trembling, blood-stained fingers for the bullet lodged somewhere between the lawman's ribs.

'I took him in, got him tried and convicted,' Buchanan said from the shadows outside the circle of bright light. 'I know he murdered his sister's husband, got his sights set on Harry Pepper's bank.'

'That's what you see on the surface,' Vaughan said through clenched teeth.

'Inside, the man's a stewpot of simmering hate laced with twisted ideas and unhealthy lusts.' He paused, his knuckles white on the hard edge of the table as the doctor muttered furiously and leaned closer.

In the shadows, Tide Buchanan sweated and patted his pockets for his tobacco sack, changed his mind, let his hand fall.

'For instance,' Vaughan continued, 'what he mentioned time and time again in the Pen was, when he got out, he was ridin' back to the Gila and he'd have the woman.'

'His sister?'

Vaughan's laugh was a shaky bark, cut off abruptly as the forceps clattered in a metal bowl and the sawbones straightened. The thin figure moved out of the light to a chiffonier. A cork popped; liquid gurgled; glass clinked against glass.

'That for you, or him?' Buchanan said, irritation creeping into his voice.

'Elizabeth Carter's maiden name was Tobyn,' Vaughan said, 'not Rachman.'

Buchanan leaned forwards, frowning. 'She's his *step*-sister?'

'Her folk took the boy in after his parents, Ben and Clare Rachman, were murdered. In time, the Tobyns died of old age. Then Elizabeth Tobyn got married to Hank

Carter, and Charlie Rachman blew his lid, lit out.'

The sawbones returned to the table, wordlessly handed a glass to Vaughan, cast a baleful glance in Buchanan's direction, then watched as the lawman threw the raw spirit down his throat and closed his eyes. Vaughan's throat worked. Sweat glistened on the white band of skin beneath his damp hair where his hat would rest.

His eyes remained closed as the agonizing probing continued. But the whiskey had put a trace of colour into his sunken cheeks, strength back into his voice.

'What Rachman kept *quiet* in the Pen,' he said, 'was his sworn oath to kill the man who led the renegades murdered his family.' His blue eyes flickered open, settled on Buchanan. 'The man you put in jail's come back to kill Cole Santee.'

'That's nonsense,' Buchanan said. He came out of his chair, moved closer to the table. 'Are you telling me Cole Santee had a hand in killing Rachman's ma and pa?'

'No, I'm not. What I am saying is a gunslinger name of *Vernon* Santee – long dead of lead poisonin' – led that gang. No relation at all to the Tumbling S rancher, but you try telling that to a kid saw his folks

104

murdered and got a name fixed in his head. Santee. It's in Rachman's records. He's sworn to kill him – and with me laid low by a slug from that owlhoot's rifle, it's up to you to get to Santee before he's blasted to perdition.'

The sawbones uttered a furious grunt. Johnny Vaughan groaned. And as a hunk of bloody metal tinkled into a shiny dish and the US Marshal's eyes rolled back in his head, Tide Buchanan swung around and walked out into the hot, clear sunlight.

TEN

It was late afternoon when they rode into the yard at Silver Spur, and the first thing Tide Buchanan did was to continue on to the low bunkhouse, slip from the saddle and slake his raging thirst with long drafts of cool, brackish water from a hide bucket hanging in the shaded doorway.

Frank Parker, a nut-brown figure coated in trail dust, was already off his horse and sniffing around the blackened ruins of the ranch house. The old hostler was dressed in blue serge pants tucked into stovepipe boots, his red galluses hooked over bony shoulders that threatened to poke through his collarless cotton shirt. The Dragoon Colt Buchanan had threatened to lock in his safe was tucked in his waistband and was heavy enough to give the serge pants a comical sag on that side.

Parker had ridden from Gila Bend astride a ragged, sway-backed paint pony that looked half dead but had threatened to outpace Buchanan's roan. On the long ride the marshal had apprised the hostler of the threat to Cole Santee's life and the different menace facing Beth Carter. Parker had shown no surprise, simply remarking that with Harry Pepper's bank also one of Wink Rachman's targets, Buchanan and his new deputy were in for a hectic time. And, the old man had added gleefully, if everything worked out right maybe they'd need the space in jail occupied by a man of the law who had been unjustly incarcerated.

That last mouthful was enough to send Parker into rasping chuckles that lasted, off and on, for more than a mile, and even caused a troubled Tide Buchanan to smile crookedly.

Now, as the marshal walked across to join the one-time army scout, Parker turned away from the mass of charred timber and let his piercing blue eyes range over the churned-up dirt of the yard.

'Take an Injun to make sense of that.'

Parker grinned without looking up. 'Ain't you never seen a blue-eyed brave?'

'No more than I've seen a white man with skin like a shrivelled apple.'

Parker grunted. 'Trackin's easy when you know how, and I've had practice.' He swung a skinny arm, said, 'There's where you rode in fast, pushin' that big roan. Santee and his crew took a different line, swung around in front of the house....'

His words trailed away as he wandered off to his left, pointed to a patch of ground further out that had been sharply cut, swung around and indicated similar sections at the far side of the yard and alongside the corral. 'That's where they rode in to do their dirty work. Came in faster than the fust time, reined in hard, then moved across to the house more leisurely.' He squinted, dropped to one knee, said, 'By then, they was leadin' a couple of riderless horses.'

'Hell,' Buchanan said in genuine disbelief, 'I must've told you that already.'

Parker spat, climbed to his feet.

'No, sir, I'm tellin' you. And I'm also tellin' you that when those fellers rode out, they left behind someone who was on one of them riderless horses, and bleedin' into the dust.'

'Young Danny Carter,' Buchanan said, his face set. 'A man don't bleed into the dirt 'less he's belly down.'

'Right here,' Parker said, pointing to a dark patch with the toe of his boot. 'And here. Then....' He lifted his gaze, his keen blue eyes drifting across the yard, finally settling on the line of cottonwoods beyond which the Gila glittered in the bright sun. 'Then they rode over to them woods.'

'Let's go.'

The air alongside the river was cool on their faces. Parker led the way along the trees, pointed once to the bloated body of a dead steer lying in flattened scrub – at which Buchanan sheered away and rode close enough to see the doctored brand without dismounting – then kneed the paint pony into the cottonwoods and threaded his way through the trees to a small clearing.

Even to Buchanan's unskilled eyes it was clear that one or more horses had spent time there. He remained in the saddle while Parker left the ragged paint to sniff around like an old dog, then rolled a cigarette and smoked it halfway down as he watched the old hostler move through the trees into the sunlight on the river bank and stand gazing into the distance.

When he returned, there was a look of satisfaction on his time-worn features.

'It's like I figured,' he said smugly.

'You mean you worked it out now – or you already knew?'

'Had a purty good idea before we left town,' Parker said.

Buchanan swore softly. 'Go on.'

'Two riders came across the Gila. Rode into the woods, joined whoever was here. Talked for a while – you can see where the horses moved around all bunched up – then they all rode off.' He jerked his thumb over his shoulder, watching Buchanan. 'Four riders. Went back across the river.' His blue eyes twinkled. 'Now, I wonder where they'd be headin'?'

'You already told me,' Buchanan said bitterly, 'yesterday. And I guess the only reason I asked you out here was to confirm what I already knew. Chug Austin's got a place in the hills, you said. If you were right, and that's where Rachman and Torres were headed when they took a shot at me, then it has to be them came back across the river last night. Rachman came down from the hills, maybe saw the house ablaze, maybe not. But right now he's got Beth Carter and Danny – and I don't think she would have gone willingly with a man she threatened to kill.'

'Riders coming,' Pedro Torres drawled.

Brush crackled as Wink Rachman wriggled to the edge of the rise, squinted down to where the trail twisted and turned through gullies and dry washes and across perilously steep slopes as it wound up towards the high ground.

Dust hung thin in the hot, still air. The metallic clink of a shod hoof was almost lost in the stillness. Then, far below, two riders emerged from behind a rocky outcrop, paused there. Bright sunlight caught their upturned faces, glinted on harness metal and on weapons.

'Buchanan,' Rachman said, his eyes on the lean figure on the larger horse.

'And?'

'Christ knows.'

Torres fondled Johnny Vaughan's shiny rifle. 'I could take them both. Without trouble.'

'No!'

'You want him for yourself?'

'Damn right I do. Santee first. Then Buchanan.'

'But Buchanan is here, now. If he keeps on coming....'

'He'll find nothing.'

Torres shrugged, looked down the slope. 'You have maybe a half-hour to make sure he doesn't.'

'Plenty for what I've got in mind,' Rachman said.

He wriggled back from the ridge, climbed to his feet and jogged down to where their horses were tethered. After a few moments, Torres followed. They walked their horses down the steep slope, then mounted up and rode at a fast gallop across the broad stretch of open grassland leading to the dark shape of Chug Austin's cabin.

'Hell,' Frank Parker said feelingly, 'that was the most goddamn foolhardy thing I've ever seen. You saw the sun flash on that rifle. Had to be Rachman or his pard. Either one of 'em could've knocked you out of the saddle.'

'He wants satisfaction,' Tide Buchanan said absently. 'Wants to look into my eyes when he pulls the trigger.'

They had topped the rise and reined in to rest their horses. Buchanan dragged a sleeve across his hot, damp face, took out his canteen, drank, tossed it to the hostler.

'Got his own private world,' he said, looking with wonder across the grassy plateau, the high, wooded slopes, the distant cabin. This fertile basin, tucked away at altitude in the Gila Bend Mountains, was not what he had expected. But as his eyes ranged along its northern flank and he saw the clear indication that someone had blocked off a box canyon, an idea that had been growing ever since Parker spoke in the saloon began to grow into a firm conviction.

'Got his own big buffalo gun,' Parker said nervously, 'and right now he could be settin' there watching us over the sights.'

'Not if that's him settin' on the stoop.'

'Yeah, well, my eyes ain't what they was,' Parker said, bridling.

'Good enough to tell if those four riders came this way?'

Parker's flashing glance was scornful. 'One horse is favourin' a hind leg. That boy's still bleedin'. We've been follerin' those same tracks all the way from the Gila.'

'So we talk to Austin.'

'A long ways to ride across open ground.'

'No other way,' Buchanan said, and lightly touched spurs to his horse's flanks.

As they neared the cabin, Chug Austin came out of his rocking chair and down the rickety steps. The big buffalo gun was dark and ugly in the crook of his arm. Buchanan looked across at Parker, grinned as the old man rolled his eyes.

Then they were in the shadows under the high trees backing the cabin and Tide Buchanan swung down and walked to meet the old reprobate.

'Must be a couple of years, Austin.'

The old man's dark eyes glittered beneath the splash of red that was his headband. 'As I recall, you took my pistol, rode me at gunpoint to the edge of town.' He chuckled at the memory. 'Next time I was in Gila, I made sure you was gone.'

'Leaving it to somebody else to throw you out,' Buchanan said, and saw Austin's lips tighten under the three-day growth of white whiskers. At the same time the old man struggled to keep his eyes fixed on Buchanan and also keep track of Frank Parker, who was down off his pony and walking in widening circles with his eyes to the ground.

Somewhere up in the hills not too far above Chug Austin's cabin, a stone rattled, and was still. And Tide Buchanan's heartbeat quickened.

'Where are they, Austin?'

'They?'

Parker came over, his eyes bright.

'This is where they rode to, all right. My guess is you'll find a lame horse in the corral – if this shack runs to such luxuries.'

Austin spat, eased the big rifle. 'My old grey went lame on me comin' down from the hills. You're welcome to take a look.'

'If it's yours,' Buchanan said, 'it'll have your brand.' And he lifted an eyebrow.

'Who needs brands,' Austin said easily, 'up here in the hills?'

Saddle leather creaked as Buchanan twisted to look back across the sunlit meadow towards the mouth of the box canyon. When he returned his gaze to Austin, the old man's eyes were guarded, the buffalo gun drifting to line up with Buchanan's belt buckle.

'We'll come to that, talk about brands and Tumbling S steers,' Buchanan said. 'First, tell me where Rachman's taken the Carters.'

Austin stared hard at Frank Parker. 'You say they was here?' He shrugged. 'Could be you're right. I'm gone most of the time. Maybe they slipped in when I was up in the hills.' He turned an injured gaze on Buchanan. 'Now you mention it, I suspicioned someone had been nosin' around, inside the cabin....'

Buchanan lifted the reins and swung away, irritated by the old man's deviousness. He rode away from the trees and the cabin, wheeled the roan to gaze up at the high ground, shielding his eyes from the harsh glare.

'Rachman!' he roared. 'Charlie Rachman!

115

We know you're up there!'

The echoes of his cry slapped away into the stillness. The hot silence settled.

'Charlie Rachman!'

A bird flapped away from the trees. The undergrowth crackled and a hundred yards away a deer burst into the open and fled gracefully, startling Buchanan so that his head snapped around and his hand slapped his holster. He cursed softly, walked the roan back into the shadows, glared in frustration at Chug Austin.

'All right,' he said tightly, 'let's talk about brands and running irons, and how last night Silver Spur was burned to the ground because a year ago I left town and an old man got thrown out of a saloon.'

Seen through a dark wall of spruce the cabin was a wooden box 500 feet down-slope, the three men on the patch of trampled ground in front of the stoop like actors mouthing silent lines on an open-air stage.

Four horses were tethered in the shade of those spruce. Two were riderless. On the other two, Beth and Danny Carter were bound and gagged. The boy sagged over hands that clung instinctively to the saddle horn. What could be seen of his face was a ghastly white. Congealed blood was thick in his matted hair, had stiffened the collar of his shirt. Lower down, under his left arm, there was a wider patch of caked blood that told of a reopened wound.

Beth Carter's blue eyes were never still. Constantly, they moved from the hunched figure of her son to the two men talking some yards away. Each time her expression changed, from one of terrible fear as she watched Danny's condition deteriorate, to another of mingled anger and hatred as she settled her gaze on Charlie Rachman.

Then a thin shout broke the stillness. Wink Rachman stepped through the trees into bright sunlight. Eyes narrowed in the dazzling glare, he watched the lean figure of the Gila Bend marshal circling his horse; heard his own name drift up to him for a second time as Tide Buchanan roared in fury; sensed Pedro Torres alongside him with his Winchester.

'Last chance, *compadre*,' Torres said softly. 'I kill him now, save you the trouble.'

'He dies at a time and place of my choosing,' Rachman said as Buchanan's cries rang out. He swung on Torres, his eyes blazing. 'This is the way it goes. Tonight, we take Cole Santee. Next thing, we take the bank. After that we ride to Casa Grande. And then we set and wait.'

Torres shook his head. 'For what we wait? A posse? You are crazy, you know. One bullet now, the man dies. Then everything else is OK – we kill this man Santee, we rob the bank, we–'

'There won't be no posse.'

'There is always a posse,' Torres said. 'Always. And now, more so; you think Buchanan will ride alone after what happened to the great Johnny Vaughan?'

'That's exactly what I do think. Because Tide Buchanan'll have a damn good reason for makin' sure he ain't forced to come after me leadin' a bunch of aggrieved townsfolk with itchy trigger fingers,' Rachman said.

Torres frowned, his dark eyes puzzled. 'We kill two men, we ride to Gila Bend and rob the bank – and this is a reason for *not* raising a posse?'

'I can't figure you, Torres,' Rachman said, heading back to the horses. 'You've been with me twenty-four hours of every day since we broke out the Pen – and you still don't get it.'

ELEVEN

Dusk was approaching when they reached the Gila River, the sun well down, the mountains to the west towering purple smudges rimmed with pink beneath skies like liquid gold.

Buchanan splashed through the water to halt on the fringe of the cottonwoods a short way from Silver Spur. Behind him came Chug Austin, sitting astride Wink Rachman's lame grey gelding, his hands lashed to the horn, his ankles secured by a rope passed beneath the horse's belly. Frank Parker brought up the rear, and as he joined Buchanan and Austin he voiced his concern.

'I could've follered 'em. Tracks was clear as daylight, headin' upslope from the cabin. And the two of us, we could've took them two pesky owlhoots.' He patted the big Dragoon tucked into his pants and scowled his disgust.

'If Rachman wants Beth, he won't harm her,' Buchanan said, investing the words with a confidence he didn't feel. 'My duty is to protect Cole Santee: yours is to take the prisoner to town.'

'And that's another thing,' Parker said, glowering at Austin. 'Only one thing cures a rustler, an' that's stretchin' his neck. Plenty of trees behind that cabin. Would've took a minute, saved all this bother.' He stared hard at Buchanan. 'Or maybe there's more to it—'

'Leave it, Frank,' Buchanan snapped.

Chug Austin laughed. 'He's gettin' scared,' he said. 'It's a long ride to Gila Bend. Thinks maybe I'll bambozzle him, get him all knotted up in his thinkin' so he cuts me free of this rawhide, lets me go.'

'Scared is right,' Parker growled, still watching Tide Buchanan. 'Scared I'll use this lass rope' – he patted the rawhide lariat dangling from his saddle – 'to hang you from the nearest tree – and being an inhabitant of these regions you'll be cognizant of the fact that the only trees around are the ones we're standin' in.'

But Tide Buchanan was only half listening. His head was cocked and Parker, who was still glaring balefully at the old rustler before gathering breath to embark on another tirade sprinkled with long words, caught his sudden tension.

Visibly, he held that deep intake of breath, his chest puffed out. Then he let it go explosively.

'Rider comin',' he said. 'From over yonder,' and he flung out an arm in the direction of the distant town.

'Get into the woods.'

Buchanan reached over for Austin's dangling reins and quickly led the grey into the shadows beneath the trees, Austin complaining loudly as his head cracked against a low branch.

Parker ignored the marshal. Buchanan watched him walk his pony along the edge of the woods, keeping well into the shadows but also retaining a good view of the approaches to Silver Spur. After a few seconds Buchanan muttered an order to Austin, quickly tied the grey's reins to a heavy branch then followed the hostler.

The setting sun cast an eerie, luminous glow over the fringes of the Gila Desert. Through that unholy yellow light a single rider was moving fast, crouched low along the neck of his speeding bronc. Three-quarters of a mile … half a mile … closing rapidly, pulling along a pall of dust that rose high to cast its own thin shadow in his wake.

When the rider was within a quarter of a mile of the two watching men and Tide Buchanan was reaching down for his Winchester, Frank Parker flashed a sudden, wide grin.

'Josh Santee.'

Buchanan grunted, straightened. 'I thought maybe it was old Judge Payne, bribed my deputy to let him out and come lookin' for some action. Knowin' his love of a scrap and the way him and Rachman are such good pals I wouldn't put it past him.' He looked sideways at the hostler. 'You telling me those eyes of yours can see his badge?'

'I know horses,' Parker said. 'So unless Josh has sold his....'

'No,' Buchanan said, squinting at the approaching rider. 'You're right. I guess something's happened in town.'

'Or maybe Josh has got word of what's happenin' out here?'

'Ain't no way he could,' Buchanan said, frowning.

But there had to be, and Buchanan knew it. Less than five minutes later, an excited Josh Santee was gasping out his tale. To dispel the boredom of guarding his dangerous prisoner, he said, he had enjoyed another lingering conversation with Gila

Bend's pretty young seamstress. When they eventually moved on to topics that were not of an intimate nature, she had innocently informed him that for at least three months, Beth Carter had known there was a threat to Cole Santee's life.

'But she didn't say nothing,' Josh explained, 'because Wink was in jail. But now he's out. So I asked Mr Hill if he'd keep an eye on the judge, and rode here as fast as I could.'

Buchanan nodded. 'You did right, Deputy,' he said, and saw the sudden look of realization and pride on the youngster's face. 'Frank's taking Chug Austin into town. I'm making for the Tumbling S, see if I can talk to your pa. I don't know how many men he can count on, this time of year....'

'Oakes, Raper, a couple more. But they'll be out, combing the scrub, counting heads.' Josh Santee frowned nervously. 'So it's up to us to make the difference, right, Marshal?'

'Looks that waay – and for your pa's sake, I hope we ain't too late.'

'Hell fire!' Josh said. 'You think maybe Rachman's already made his move?'

'At a time like this,' Buchanan said grimly, 'thinkin' of any kind ain't much help.' He turned to the hostler. 'You all set?'

'Ain't got no choice,' Parker grumbled.

'One thing,' Buchanan said. 'Before you go, Frank – hand over that rope.'

'Aw, heck, Tide–'

'Do it!'

With a muttered curse, Parker, freed the rawhide lariat and tossed in a looping throw to Buchanan. He secured it to his saddle, watched the hostler make his way into the woods to emerge moments later leading Chug Austin's grey, then turned to Josh Santee.

'Right, Deputy. Let's ride.'

Darkness descended when they were no more than halfway to Santee's spread, unrolling behind them from the east like a vast unstoppable blanket intent on enveloping and extinguishing the last golden rays of the sun.

With it came a terrible premonition. It was as if the blackness of night had crept in to enfold Tide Buchanan's soul in a suffocating embrace that banished all hope, and the foreboding that convinced him Charlie Rachman had stolen a march on him was made all the worse for having Cole Santee's son along, excitedly riding at his stirrup.

With that black tide of despair there came

the nagging suspicion that Frank Parker had been right, the excuse Buchanan had given him all wrong. It was not his duty to protect Cole Santee. As a lawman, his priority was to recapture the escaped convicts and free hostages. That he had ignored that responsibility and deliberately turned his back and ridden away to protect a man who was not only several miles distant but well capable of looking after himself was, surely, a dereliction of duty.

So, why had he done it?

It stemmed, Buchanan supposed glumly, from a feeling of guilt. He had long admitted to himself that Beth Carter was the woman he wanted alongside him for the rest of his life. But it had always troubled him that those feelings had been clear to most people – and certainly to Beth – for some time before Charlie Rachman rode into Gila Bend, six months ago, on his way to Silver Spur.

And that was where the guilt came in. Buchanan knew Rachman, knew his reputation, had known instinctively that no good could come from his ride to Spur. That he had let him go without hindrance smacked of opportunism. Charlie Rachman was unbalanced, and a dangerous gunman. Hank

Carter was Beth's husband, and so stood in Buchanan's way. If Rachman rode to Spur, got involved in an argument and ended up killing Carter, all problems would be solved. Beth would be free, and Buchanan could tidy all the loose ends by arresting Charlie Rachman.

Tide Buchanan shuddered, gazing bleakly and unseeingly ahead as he and Josh Santee thundered towards the Tumbling S.

So now, because of that guilt – which, surely, was unproven and quite possibly a figment of his own heated imagination – he had left Beth Carter. Not wanting to compound the guilt by being seen to favour the woman, he had turned his back on her.

And Frank Parker knew what he had done; had given him the chance to change his mind and go back – and Buchanan had ignored it–

'Gunfire,' Josh Santee shouted. 'I heard shots.'

Buchanan's jaw tightened. Above the drum of hooves he heard, again, the distant crackle of gunfire.

'Did you bring along a Winchester?' he yelled.

'No, I guess it kinda slipped my mind,' the boy called back.

And as young Josh Santee thundered past him, his face shining with supreme confidence and the famous old Colt Paterson clutched in his fist, Buchanan had a hunch that, even with both those noble assets added together and reinforced with the weight of his own formidable presence, they didn't have enough to save Cole Santee.

It was in Buchanan's mind that when they reached the Tumbling S they would find Cole Santee's big house under siege, with Wink Rachman and his 'breed pard laying down a withering fire with their saddle guns under cover of which the two owlhoots would inch their way forward and strive to gain entry.

He was wrong.

The marshal and his deputy cut the frantic pace of their horses as they came in sight of the ranch buildings, stood tall in the stirrups as they strained to see across the big corral. But the thickening darkness of night was already being ripped apart by the leaping flames that licked at the trees above the blazing bunkhouse, casting shifting pools of flickering light over the two inert bodies lying in the dust of the yard.

'They've fired the bunkhouse, made it into

the house,' Josh Santee said in a fearful, husky voice, and it was with a sinking heart that Tide Buchanan listened to the crack of gunfire and knew that the boy was right.

The door to the ranch house gaped. Even as they passed the three horses left ground-hitched by the owlhoots and drew near, an oil lamp crashed to the floor and bright flame erupted in a rolling cloud of thick black smoke. A shotgun blasted. One window exploded outwards in a shower of glass, and over the roar of flames and the dying echoes of the shotgun's roar, a man laughed.

Cole Santee's shotgun; Wink Rachman's crazy laughter.

Buchanan's jaw tightened. He rode past the body of the wrangler, Wes Lake, let his eyes sweep across the other dead or dying man without recognition, then turned his attention to the house and went into action.

'This is the law,' he roared, hurling himself out of the saddle and drawing his six-gun as he sprinted, crouching, for the steps. 'Rachman, Torres, throw down your hoglegs and come out with your hands up.'

He flung himself down, panting, alongside the steps, poked out his six-gun and fired twice into the air, his body below the level of the gallery's floor. As he did so the same crazy laugh rang out, causing Buchanan's skin to prickle. A shot rang out, from close to the open door, and dirt spouted between Josh Santee's boots as he dived for cover at the other side of the steps.

'Pa! Are you OK!'

The boy's yell was lost in the growing crackle of flames, the sudden burst of gunfire as the two men inside the burning room – dark shapes against the leaping flames – launched themselves into an attack that took them deep into the house beyond the fire and out of sight.

Buchanan's next two hastily triggered shots sent lead thumping harmlessly into the room's back wall.

With a cry of despair, Josh Santee came up in an agile leap that took him in one bound to the top of the steps. He was already halfway across the gallery and making for the door when Buchanan rose to fling himself forwards in a headlong dive and catch the boy's ankle with his straining, outstretched hand. The boards shook as Santee stretched his length. He twisted furiously, kicked away from Buchanan and came up on his feet.

But now Buchanan was ahead of him, and

stronger. He leaped forwards and slammed the boy against the wall, bracing his legs and holding the deputy there with the weight behind his shoulder.

'There's no way through,' he snapped, and brought his hand up to hold the struggling boy's face still with iron fingers, then twist it so that the wide eyes reflected the dancing flames. 'You go in that way you'll be burned to a cinder – you hear me!'

'My pa–!'

'If he's got sense, he's out the back way. But there's only one way to find out.'

'Dammit, all right!'

Santee went still. Buchanan held him a moment longer – then stepped back. He said, 'Both of us. That fire's workin' for us. Nobody's comin' out through this door.'

He stiff armed the boy, sent him stumbling along the gallery, followed hastily as Santee came to his senses and vaulted the rail into darkness. With Buchanan close behind him he moved swiftly along the windowless side wall of the house.

In the shadow of that wall, time seemed to stand still, while all around the world moved on. It could only have taken a matter of seconds to run from the gallery to the rear of the house, but in what was little more than a blink of an eye Buchanan heard the shotgun blast, heard the fierce rattle of six-gun fire, heard the desperate cry of a man cornered and heard that cry change to a sudden groan of agony that died in a liquid gurgle which was itself drowned by an explosion of laughter.

Then they were around the wall. With eyes made night-blind by the dazzling light of the fires, they walked into blackness.

Running footsteps faded away into the darkness. Undergrowth crackled, and Buchanan thought he heard a feminine gasp followed by a sudden cry of distress that caused the hair on his nape to prickle.

Suddenly, Josh cried out.

Eyes were becoming accustomed to the darkness, helped by flames that had now burst through the roof of the house to send sparks erupting through the trees. Buchanan swore softly, stood stock still.

'It's Pa,' Josh said.

He was crouched over the bulky form that had flopped across the step and blocked his way, brought him to his knees as he stumbled into its solid weight. As Buchanan moved to stand alongside he saw that the boy's hands were wet with blood, and one glance into Cole Santee's glassy, staring eyes told the marshal that there was no life in the big rancher.

'Josh....'

He turned away, sickened, heard the sound of men thrashing through the woods and knew that Rachman and Torres, their terrible work done, were circling around, making for the horses in the yard.

But ... three horses?'

'With me, Deputy,' Buchanan snapped, using the official term partly as a deliberate ploy to wrench the boy away from the body of his father, partly because if there were three owlhoots, then he would need the youngster's help.

But even as the thoughts sped through his mind and he turned away and raced to retrace his steps around the side of the burning house, he was recalling the soft feminine gasp of fear. And he knew that, for cowards such as Wink Rachman, a hostage was a shield that diverted the minds of pursuers, weakened their resolve and left them in turmoil.

It wouldn't work, Buchanan vowed. It *couldn't* work, if he was to retain confidence in his own ability as a lawman; if he was to return to Gila Bend and face US Marshal

Johnny Vaughan with his head held high and....

And with Beth Carter safe and well.

Then he had reached the corner of the house and the yard was in front of him, awash in a sea of dancing light and shadow that lapped at the three riders and gave them the appearance of movement even though they were still.

Rachman, Torres – and Beth Carter, her horse tight up against the 'breed's, the gleaming Winchester held at an angle by Torres so that its muzzle probed the soft flesh at the base of the woman's throat.

And again Tide Buchanan's mind seemed to shift. If three riders, why not four? If Beth was there, where was Danny?

Even as his mind balked, as it sheered away from the horror of what the boy's absence must mean, Josh Santee came up behind him, panting, and across the yard Wink Rachman's laughter rang out.

'Take your time, Buchanan,' he roared. 'You're lettin' us go because, unless you ride fast to Chug Austin's spread, that boy'll die.'

'And you?' Buchanan yelled. 'Do I save the boy, so's you can kill the woman?'

'Beth's my insurance,' Rachman shouted. 'She stays with me for sure until we're clear,

133

maybe longer if I'm so inclined. You come after me, hell, that's your business. But you come ridin' with a posse, and this girl gets a slug through the head!'

The laugh rang through the night, and over it Beth Carter's broken voice cried out, choked with tears.

'Go to Danny, Tide. He's ... he's all I've got, and if he doesn't make it–'

'All right!' Buchanan stepped into the garish light, lifted his hands wide, clear of his holster. 'All right, Beth. I'll see to it. But you, Rachman....'

He shook his head lost for words, held up his stiff arm as a barrier as the glint of a drawn pistol caught the corner of his eye and Josh Santee made as if to push past.

'There ain't enough miles you can ride,' Buchanan said, 'to stay ahead of me. There ain't a horse can carry you far enough, there ain't a hostage you can take'd keep you safe.' His voice was quiet, but filled with a deadly purpose that carried it above the fierce crackle of burning timber. 'You're dead, Rachman. In Arizona, in Texas, in any territory you make for, in any state you can reach – that woman dies and you cross that river to perdition.'

And as the words faded away and the

owlhoots with their hostage rode away from Silver Spur, Buchanan took a deep breath, spoke gruffly to Josh Santee and made swiftly for his horse.

TWELVE

In the blackened stove the resiny wood hissed and crackled, the fire rapidly turning the metal cherry-red and sending fierce billows of smoke and heat through the filthy cluttered cabin. In no time at all the sweat was streaming from Tide Buchanan and his young deputy, but on the iron cot at the back of the room the injured Danny Carter lay with chattering teeth and a face that glistened wet and white as bone.

They had ridden from the Tumbling S to Chug Austin's cabin to find the door open, the boy sprawled across the threshold leaking blood into the filthy dirt floor and with his black hair glistening in the cold light of the moon. Young Josh Santee, fresh from staring at the body of his dead father and with the prospect of a fierce gun battle with two desperate owlhoots not too far ahead of him, had gone silent, his own face pale. Nevertheless, he had set to with a will, helping Buchanan carry Carter inside, then swiftly gathering kindling and logs to build a fire in the stove.

Once a tin pot of scalding hot water was steaming and bubbling, Buchanan had changed the dressing on the unconscious boy's bullet-scored ribs, decided with the benefit of long experience in such matters that the inflammation was angry but not dangerous, then turned his attention to the scalp wound.

The puffed, bruised flesh, the ugly lacerations and the glassy look in the boy's eyes when he drifted in and out consciousness suggested something a damn sight more serious than a flesh wound across the ribs. Nevertheless, Buchanan judged, if there was no skull fracture then it was a wound that would heal itself, given time and rest. Without doubt the boy was concussed, and needed a doctor. But the doctor was a long, hard ride away, such a trip would do more harm than good, and it was Buchanan's opinion that – more than anything else – the tension and excitement of the past few hours were the major causes of Danny Carter's condition.

'Wore himself out,' he said, pulling the grubby animal skins over the boy as Josh came over to the cot. 'Got himself all worked up, needed rest after Oakes's slug knocked him down. Didn't get it, and that whack across the head's sapped what strength he had left, laid him low.'

'He surely ain't goin' nowhere,' Josh said.

'That he ain't,' Buchanan agreed, tight-lipped. 'And with Rachman and Torres headed fast towards town, takin' his ma with them, the best thing we can do for Danny Carter is leave him be, let him rest up here.'

'You reckon they're aimin' to rob the bank?' Josh asked, and Buchanan laughed mirthlessly.

'Harry Pepper don't open for business until ten,' he said, 'and by that time those two gunslingers'll be in the Gila Bend jail – or halfway to Texas.'

'No, sir, they ain't getting' away,' Josh Santee said, his face set, his eyes hard. 'They killed my pa, gunned down Matt Oakes and the best damn wrangler my pa ever saw. I'll settle with them if I have to ride clear to … to….'

'Yeah,' Buchanan said, his mind on Beth Carter, 'I know the feeling.' He cocked a quizzical eyebrow at the deputy. 'If that was Oakes alongside Wes Lake, where the hell was Vince Raper?'

'I wondered about that,' Josh Santee said,

'but I ain't too surprised if he saw trouble comin' and drifted. He was always first in line to collect his monthly pay, but he never did seem a part of Tumbling S.'

'Yeah, well....' Buchanan reflected for a moment on the dark eyed, unshaven gun-slinger, decided that he was the last man he'd expect to run away from trouble, then clapped Santee on the shoulder, spun him about.

'Danny's as comfortable as we can make him, got water to drink when he wakes up. Ain't a thing more we can do here, and time's runnin' out.'

'We ride?' There was so much eagerness in Santee's voice that it dragged a grin from Buchanan.

'We ride,' he confirmed, and watched with considerable astonishment as his young deputy fairly leaped out of the cabin.

They rode fast across the moonlit desert, balancing necessary haste against the need to conserve their horses' strength, con-stantly fretting and fuming at the knowledge that the owlhoots' three-hour start had put them too far ahead to be caught. Buch-anan's sole aim was to ensure the gap between them did not widen. When Josh

Santee begged for more speed, Buchanan snapped terse orders to hold him back, then stoically endured the hot lash of his infuriated young deputy's tongue.

Once, by the light of the moon, they stopped alongside a stand of parched trees to drink thirstily from their canteens and looked with considerable misgivings at their horses' heaving flanks. A brief wet from water tipped into upturned stetsons moistened their sticky, foam streaked muzzles, but when Santee made as if to climb back into the saddle, Buchanan held him back and wandered out into the bright moonlight to walk back and forth across the wide trail with head bent.

'I'm no tracker,' he said, returning to the trees to light up a cigarette and trickle smoke, 'and there's been so much to-ing and fro-ing between Gila Bend and Silver Spur I guess Frank Parker's the only man I know could accurately unravel the signs. But from what I can make out,' he said thoughtfully, 'two riders rode to town, and they were followed by three more.'

'Parker and Austin, then those owlhoots and my ma,' Josh Santee said, watching Buchanan, knowing there was more to come.

'Right. But there's also sign of another rider,' Buchanan said. 'I ain't smart enough to say when he rode this way – before, after, or smack in the middle of them others – but it's easy to see he was pushing his horse hard, making for Gila Bend and in one hell of a hurry.'

'Vince Raper,' Santee said.

'Maybe it was,' Buchanan conceded, 'and maybe all he's doin' is gettin' clear of trouble. But that don't make sense. He was in the thick of things last time I saw him at Silver Spur, could've lit out then, but didn't. I never had him pegged as the kind of feller to be fazed by a couple of losers like Rachman and Torres – and, as I recall, when your pa got the news of the Yuma jail break, Raper didn't blink an eye.'

'Now you mention it,' Josh Santee said, 'I got the impression that all Raper was doin' at Tumblin' S was passing time.'

Buchanan grunted, let the words drift around in his mind so that their sinister portent could maybe settle and make some kind of sense – then took a deep breath and shrugged away the gloom.

'Which is what we're doin' right now,' he said. 'Passing time we can't spare.'

'Hell, that ain't my doing!' Santee said

hotly, and Buchanan turned away, grinning, to climb into the saddle.

'Think about this,' he shouted as they kicked their horses into a gallop. 'If Vince Raper is in cahoots with Rachman and Torres – what the hell's he doin' ridin' like a madman for Gila Bend?'

THIRTEEN

They rode into town with the low morning sun searing their eyes and their throats parched by the dust of the desert, saw through slitted eyelids the way the dazzling sunlight was casting the long, restless shadows of the cluster of men on horseback outside the saloon and glinting on weapons that were already loose in worn holsters or resting across the thick thighs of townsmen who sat tense and nervous in the saddle.

Angry voices growled words that were lost in the general muttering of discontent; a barked laugh lacked any vestige of humour, chilling with its latent cruelty; and suddenly, shockingly, a gunshot sounded, restless horses were startled into movement and began milling, riders cursed the man who had carelessly pulled the trigger, unshaven faces flashed pale in the light of the sun as first one, then another, turned and caught sight of the approaching lawmen.

Spencer Hill was talking to Frank Parker on the plankwalk outside Buchanan's office, a Winchester in the crook of his arm. He sensed the change in the waiting men's demeanour, caught the sound of approaching hoofbeats, whirled quickly and at once gestured urgently to Buchanan.

The marshal and his deputy swung in to the rail, dismounted and hitched their dust-caked horses, and were at once drowned in a torrent of rapid-fire talk from an excited Frank Parker that used up a deal of free-flying spittle, said a lot but told them nothing.

'Easy, now,' Buchanan said. He flicked a glance at the jail, and to calm down the old hostler said quietly, 'First things first, Frank. Did you manage to get Chug Austin to jail, or did you leave him somewhere back down the trail with his face all black and swollen?'

'You know damn well you took away my lass rope, Marshal,' Parker growled, hitching at serge pants that still sagged under the weight of the big Dragoon pistol. 'Austin's locked up all snug next door to the judge, but that don't mean he's safe. 'Less you move fast, that posse'll bust him out and string him up before they ride hell for leather after the men robbed Harry Pepper's bank, rode away with a gunny-sack stuffed with cash money.'

'Jesus!' young Josh Santee breathed. 'I'd best break out the shotguns, get–'

'Wait.' Buchanan lifted a hand, glanced from Parker to Spencer Hill. 'How come the bank, Spence? Has Harry Pepper taken to workin' all night?'

'Not of his own accord,' Hill said. His brow was furrowed, and Buchanan knew he was thinking deeper than the old hostler, was certainly sharp enough – if he had seen her – to realize the implications of Beth Carter riding with the owlhoots. 'That black-eyed gunslinger from Tumblin' S hammered in before dawn, roused Harry by kickin' down his door, then forced him at gunpoint to bring that big bunch of keys into town. I'd been out back talkin' to the judge, stepped out for fresh air and a smoke. Damn feller blasted a shot sprayed me with splinters. I ducked back, but by the time I'd grabbed me a rifle and stepped out again the bank was open, and Rachman and another feller were climbin' down off their horses.'

'No sign of Beth?'

'Jesus! – Beth Carter? She's with Rach-man?'

'Hostage,' Buchanan said. 'Rachman's

usin' her to make damn sure I don't go after him with a posse. I'm the man who got him a life stretch in Yuma, ain't that what you said, Spence? A posse'd spoil his personal vendetta, not to mention maybe fillin' him full of holes and ruinin' his chance of gettin' even.' He shrugged. 'If they didn't bring her into town, they must have left her safe somewheres, tied up and gagged so she couldn't holler, but for sure he's going to use her.'

He broke off. Three horsemen had detached themselves from the group outside the saloon. They rode at a walk down the street, and Buchanan stepped to the edge of the plankwalk as he recognized Evans, the rail-thin leader of the town council, alongside him the swarthy figure of the blacksmith, with the pale, moustachioed saloonist, Ed McMahon, bringing up the rear.

One petty official: two habitual trouble-makers.

'Climb down,' Buchanan called as they drew near, then deliberately turned his back without listening to the reply. Quietly, to Hill and Parker, he said, 'I'll deal with this alone, in the office, put it on an official footing. But you two stick close, keep your ears open. These three are the heart and soul of the posse. Without them, it'll fall apart, break up.'

When the three men stepped into the office, stamping dust from their boots, he was seated behind the desk, Josh Santee off to one side with a haunch on the desk and his vest swept back to reveal his deputy's badge. Two of the party wore six-guns, awkwardly, in holsters that were stiff from disuse. The blacksmith toted a shotgun. All three armed men brought with them the rank smell of sweat, and Buchanan knew that their tension came from uncertainty and no small measure of fear. He also knew their fear would work for him: common sense was unlikely to prevail, but a sudden show of strength would provide them with the excuse of being forced, against their will and to their collective moral indignation, to back off.

'Before you begin,' he said, 'who raised that posse?'

'I took it upon myself to act,' Evans said stiffly, 'seeing as the lawman we employ to protect us was out of town.'

'No doubt over at Silver Spur, spendin' a cosy evenin' with his lady friend,' the blacksmith said with a sneer.

Buchanan ignored him. Still looking hard at the skinny town official he said, 'You raised it, Mr Evans, you can now stand the men down. There'll be no posse.'

'When they robbed Pepper, they took my money.' The saloonist's jaw jutted under his drooping moustache. 'I'll go after what's mine.'

'Rachman and Torres murdered Cole Santee,' Buchanan said, and saw the shock register, the swift glances directed at young Josh, the sudden realization that the boy was wearing a badge. 'If they can gun down a powerful rancher backed by a tough crew,' he said, 'you think you townsfolk stand a chance?'

'We can try,' Evans said, but his face had lost some colour as the bluster began to leak out of his boots.

'The easy way, or the hard way,' Buchanan said. 'Call off the posse – or I'll do it for you.'

'They won't listen,' the blacksmith growled. 'Every man jack of 'em's lost money, and if you ain't with us–'

'Hell,' said the saloonist, 'we're wastin' time–'

'And gamblin' with Pepper's life!' The blacksmith leaned forward to slam his

148

meaty fist on Buchanan's desk. 'They're playin' with us, Marshal. Took Harry Pepper along with his head in a noose, that bastard Rachman laughin' fit to bust when he told us they was headed for Casa Grande. Now if that ain't reason enough to raise a posse of good, honest men who ain't scared–'

'You're not listening.' Buchanan's eyes were bleak. 'A posse means you're playin' into *Rachman's* hands, givin' him all the excuse he needs–'

'Oh, for Christ's sake–'

'Spence, Frank!'

At Buchanan's sharp call the door slammed open.

The saloonist slapped his holster, turned, froze. The blacksmith faced the door, stepped to one side. Moving fast for his bulk he lifted the shotgun, then thought better of it as he saw he was covered by Hill's Winchester and the hostler's deadly Dragoon. Behind him, Buchanan deliberately cocked his six-gun, and the blacksmith visibly sagged.

'No!' The councillor's voice was thin with panic.

'It's over,' Buchanan said, climbing out of his chair. 'Frank, Spence, take these three out back, hold them in the cell block, stay with them.' He moved around the desk, said to Josh Santee, 'You're in charge, Deputy. I'm takin' a walk down the street. Stay by the door until that posse disperses. When that happens, call the others, let these damn fool citizens go.'

He went out onto the plankwalk and in the intensifying morning heat strode purposefully towards the saloon. His boots thudded. Dust puffed up from beneath his feet, drifted into the sunlit street. The cluster of men fell silent as he approached. A horse snorted. Bridle metal jingled.

Without pausing, Tide Buchanan said, 'It's over, fellers. Go on home.' And as he moved on, passing Harry Pepper's bank, passing the town seamstress's neat premises, drawing near to the brass shingle on the wall marking the judge's office, the sudden break in tension was palpable. He heard a laugh that was rich with relief, a surly objection that was stamped out before it developed into an argument, the sound of horses moving away at a walk, in all directions.

But their tension was now his. And before he could go after Wink Rachman, he had one more chore.

His knock was answered at once by a

woman who peered around the half-open door and wore a look that was at once belligerent and contrite – if that were possible.

'Agnes,' Buchanan said, 'I think it's time the judge came home.'

'You think you can trust me?'

'I reckon anger dies, given time. Ed's always been a philanderer, and I guess his last fling – 'specially as it was with that sassy Belle over at the saloon – was hard to take. I locked him up for his own protection because you were … not yourself. But if I can be sure he won't get his fool head blown off by a woman totin'–'

'Go get him.' Agnes Payne, neé, Smallbone, fully opened the door alongside the gleaming brass shingle she had continued to polish with loving care while the husband she had sworn to kill reclined in the safety of his strap-steel cell, and handed Tide Buchanan an old, battered shotgun. 'Show him that. Let him hold it. He knows it's the only weapon available, discounting carving knives and such. Tell him….'

Buchanan waited.

'Oh, heavens, just tell him to come on home,' she finished and, as she closed the door with a bang, Buchanan was almost certain her thin face was suffused by a shy blush.

When he turned away, his own face had hardened.

The posse had dispersed. Josh Santee was ushering his three temporary prisoners out of the jailhouse, and Spencer Hill and Frank Parker were heading towards their respective businesses.

It was time to release Ed Payne, check on Johnny Gaunt's health, then ride to the inevitable showdown with Wink Rachman at Casa Grande.

FOURTEEN

Marshal Tide Buchanan and his young deputy, Josh Santee, rode through the rest of that long morning and on into the searing heat of the afternoon, pushing on hard in an easterly direction, riding with the merciless sun a dead weight beating down on their heads and the nearest shade the cotton-woods lining the Gila River some twenty miles to the north. They talked only sporadically, each man alone with his thoughts, each in his own way confronting nameless fears.

For Buchanan that task was soon done, for he had long ago learned that a man's worst fears were frequently groundless, dark figments of an unfettered and unreasoning imagination that always seemed hell-bent on seeking out the worst and using those horrors to sap a man's strength and will.

As far as he could tell from occasional sidelong glances, Josh Santee was also bearing up well, and it was with a whimsical inner smile that Buchanan admitted that

153

there was considerable benefit to be gained from being young and inexperienced. Youth went into battle with an unshakeable belief in their own invincibility and the conviction that their opponents were incompetent fools. If recklessness could be curbed, that sanguineness gave them a huge advantage. Battles were won in the mind. A man who believed he could be beaten – or whose mind sheered away from the awesome and awful tasks he must face – would do well to stay out of the fray. So ponderings on a man's possible mental fragility occupied Buchanan's mind as they rode on through the blistering Arizona heat; he thought long and hard about the half-crazy Wink Rachman, and sought for ways to push the gunman over the edge.

'He'll be expectin' us to ride straight at him,' he said after a while.

'Ride in with guns blazin'?' Santee, immediately following his chief's line of thought, squinted across and nodded. 'But then all him and Torres'll do is hide behind them two hostages.'

'So we sneak up on 'em,' Buchanan said. 'Take 'em by surprise.'

Santee grinned. 'Last time I asked, you said we'd be at Casa Grande in an hour. Still broad daylight, Marshal. What d'you aim to do, make us invisible?'

'That's *exactly* what I aim to do,' Buchanan said, 'by makin' use of all the hard work them Hohokam Injuns did for us more than a thousand years ago.' Under the shade of a lifted hand he gazed past Josh Santee to the north-east, saw on the far horizon the low smudge of greenery that, until that precise moment, had not figured in his plans, and nodded his satisfaction.

'Swing your horse that way, Deputy,' he said, gesturing towards the distant strip of vegetation. 'What *you* see over yonder is a stretch of trees alongside a long-dead canal. What I see is the side entrance to Casa Grande.'

They cut across country in the new north-easterly direction, unavoidably lengthening the time it would take them to reach the Hohokams' ancient adobe watchtower but, to Buchanan's way of thinking, ensuring that they got there unobserved and with their hides unperforated.

'And that,' he said, voicing his thoughts, 'is good for both hostages. Ain't no damn use us gettin' there all shot to pieces.'

'Small risk,' Santee said, twisting sideways

in the saddle to spit dust. 'Rachman wants you for himself. He ain't going to knock you out of the saddle from half a mile away, miss all the fun of watchin' you die.'

'Well, thank you, young Josh.' Buchanan grinned across at his deputy. 'You're right about Rachman, but it'd be too damn easy for Torres to take himself all the way to the fourth floor and give himself a fine view clear across the desert. I already know from experience one of them fellers is trigger happy, and my money's on the 'breed.'

'You always waste time talkin' about something that ain't going to happen?'

'Shows I'm nervous,' Buchanan said. 'Now, come on, Deputy, let's you and me do some serious ridin'.'

It took them the best part of an hour to reach what was left of the irrigation canal those Indians of long ago had constructed to carry life-giving water a full seventeen miles from the Gila River to their settlement at Casa Grande. The line of cottonwoods Buchanan had pointed out to Santee proved to be a deceptive landmark, despite the riders' feverish haste, remaining fixed in the distance for what seemed an eternity until, to both riders' relief, it grew in size and definition, took shape and form so that the cool grey-green of individual leaves could clearly be seen, the ranks of trees promising welcome relief from the burning heat of the desert.

But the cruel deception did not end there. As they rode wearily out of the dust and the heat it became clear that cottonwoods that had looked so inviting from a distance were surviving precariously on traces of water that trickled far below the rock-hard surface of the land. The trees afforded some meagre shade but were sparse and stunted, their leaves parched and withered. The old water-course was clearly marked, but the centuries had reduced it to a derelict, arid channel, where sun-loving snakes basked and lizards darted, tails flicking, among stones and tangled mesquite.

'Just about enough cover there for a man crawlin' on his belly, if he don't mind facin' angry rattlers,' Josh Santee said disappointedly, snatching off his Stetson and dashing the dust-caked sweat from his brow.

'Not exactly what I had in mind,' Buchanan said equably, 'but close enough.'

Santee's eyes widened. 'You mean you plan on goin' in on foot?'

'All the way,' Buchanan said. 'Even then

we can't be certain of catchin' them by surprise. A man high up in that adobe can keep a watch in most directions. He'd need to be blind not to spot the dust we've been trailin' all the way from Gila Bend.'

He folded his hands on the horn, leaned forward, let the words sink in and waited patiently for the boy's reaction.

Santee was down from the saddle, stretching his legs, digging into his saddle-bags. He found his canteen, uncorked, took a long swig. With water trickling down his chin and dribbling onto his shirt-front he said, 'But surely that'll work for us? Riders headin' away from them'll be no concern. They'll dismiss that dust trail, keep lookin' for someone headin' straight as an arrow for Casa Grande.'

'I knew I did right pinnin' that badge on your shirt,' Tide Buchanan said approvingly. 'Yeah, you're right, Josh. My aim in headin' this way was not only so's we could attack from an unexpected direction, but to make sure them two owlhoots'll be lookin' the wrong way when we do.'

'Always supposin',' Santee said slyly, 'that Rachman ain't as clever as me – because if he is, he'll have second-guessed you, Marshal.'

'Then I'll second-guess him right back,' Buchanan said, slipping out of the saddle. 'With the way in across the desert empty as a starving man's tin plate, Rachman'll expect us to sneak up under cover of darkness. I intend to disillusion him.'

Santee slammed home the cork with his palm, slipped the canteen inside his shirt and squinted with obvious misgivings at the winding course of the old Indian waterway as it arrowed across the desert. Then, with a shrug of his shoulders, he followed Buchanan's example, walked his horse to the best shade he could find and quickly fitted hobbles to its forelegs.

Buchanan was well aware that the sun was dipping towards the distant hills, the shadows of the cottonwoods lengthening. Working fast he located his own canteen, checked the loads of Winchester and six-gun, dug the carton of extra shells out of his saddle-bags. As an afterthought, he unfastened the thong securing Chug Austin's lass rope and looped the thirty-foot rawhide lariat over his shoulder. Then, satisfied that he'd got all he needed, he gave the big blue roan a reassuring slap. It snorted, nudged the marshal with its shoulder, then tossed its head and moved off into the trees.

'Ready?'

'As ever will be,' Josh Santee said. His voice was tight.

Prepared to move off, Buchanan caught the boy's tone and sought to offer words of encouragement. 'The most deceptive light a man can work in,' he said, 'is between daylight and darkness.'

'Doesn't that affect everyone the same?'

'Yeah. But Rachman and Torres'll have raw eyes from gazin' for hours over the white dust of the desert. Dusk comes, every dip in the land'll hide a man with a gun, every shadow'll move.'

'And all we've got to do,' Santee said, as Tide Buchanan set off along the edge of the ancient watercourse, 'is to get two slick gunmen out of a building affords them all the cover they need – and do it before they kill both hostages.'

'Put like that,' Buchanan tossed over his shoulder with a grin, 'it's as easy as fallin' off a log.'

Buchanan estimated that their fast ride had intersected the Hohokam waterway some five miles from Casa Grande, leaving an awesome task ahead for men accustomed to sitting comfortably in the saddle. Knowing

160

that time was running out they covered the first two miles at a steady jog, but both lawmen were quickly gasping and drenched in sweat as they stuck to the unfamiliar gait for which high-heeled cowboy boots were unsuitable, over terrain that was both uneven and tangled with undergrowth that snagged boots and clothing and several times brought them to their knees.

After Josh Santee had crashed down for the third time, Buchanan called a halt.

They rested, drank the last of their water, sent empty canteens clattering hollowly into the watercourse. While Josh Santee sank down against the bole of a tree, Stetson pushed back from his flushed face as he gathered strength, Buchanan strode out of the cottonwoods into the cooling light of the sun and looked anxiously to the south.

The adobe of Casa Grande was clearly visible, an off-white structure from which jutted the broken bones of old timber beams, rearing high against the flaming evening skies. Even as he watched, the marshal saw light flash on metal in a dark rectangle that was one of the upper windows; thought he heard a whisper of sound that could have been a man's voice drifting on the clear, thin air.

But just as it had when they first came across the desert towards the cottonwoods, the flat, featureless landscape was making a mockery of distance. The crumbling walls of Casa Grande appeared to loom close, but there was still some way to go. Conscious of the weariness in his own body, knowing that, with all its advantages, youth couldn't match the stamina of a grown man toughened by years of action, Buchanan set his jaw and returned to his young deputy.

'Like I thought, they're watchin' from the top windows.'

'Pepper and Beth Carter too, you reckon?'

'Only one way of findin' out.' Buchanan hitched his gunbelt, spat. 'You ready?'

'Sure thing.'

The voice was pained, disgusted that the marshal would suggest otherwise. And so they pressed on.

There was blood on both men's shirts when, what must have been a full half-hour later, Buchanan touched Santee's shoulder and finally called a halt. Their clothing was torn by the cruel mesquite, their senses numbed by the effort of will that had driven them on through exhaustion and pain. They had stumbled over razor-sharp rocks, fought their way through undergrowth bristling

162

with needle thorns – had once, out of sheer desperation when the thickets of mesquite became impenetrable, moved out of the trees and risked discovery for fifteen minutes of easier going on the fringes of the desert.

But now they were within fifty yards of Casa Grande. And, down on one knee at the edge of the stunted trees, Buchanan could see the four horses loose-hitched behind the adobe, the watercourse carrying on for some way beyond the building before petering out, its usefulness at an end.

'Served them Indians – now it's served us,' he said to Santee as he ducked back under cover. 'But gettin' this far is just the beginning. Those hostages put us in a bind, rule out any possibility of an open assault. We do that, they'll die.'

'A lot of rooms in that place,' Santee said. 'Two men can't keep watch on every damn one of them.'

'The more you talk, the more sense you make, Deputy.' Buchanan slipped Austin's lass rope off his shoulder, hefted the coils. 'I guess you already figured out what this is for?'

'I know what springs to mind. As a youngster I was always throwin' a loop over a high branch, usin' the rope for a swing – or for a way up.'

'Gettin' into Casa Grande that way'll be risky, and hard going. But with covering fire, the man who climbs up there'll stand a good chance of makin' it.'

'Are we flippin' a coin – or have you already decided who's gonna shin up that rope?'

Buchanan took a breath, let it out. 'Those hostages are my responsibility, Josh.'

'Added to which,' Santee said, 'you've got a personal interest in Beth Carter.' The young deputy shook his head. 'I'm not sure this is the right way. Didn't you tell me those owlhoots were watchin' from the high windows?'

Buchanan nodded. He shared Santee's misgivings. From a distance he had seen the rays of the setting sun flashing on the barrel of a rifle high in the building. There were four floors; as far as he could recall, eleven rooms. There was no reason for the gunman to come down from the upper floor until full darkness. The uncertainty lay in knowing the location of the second man, and the hostages. If one man was on the upper floor, what did that make the odds on guessing right about the other three – with lives forfeited if he was wrong?

'The only thing certain is there was a man at the top of the building. That watercourse goes straight on behind the adobe. Take my Winchester. Soon as I've snaked along so's I'm level with the back wall, start sendin' slugs in through that top window.'

'All right,' Santee said, accepting Buchanan's saddle gun and spare shells. 'That'll wake him up, but then what?'

'Neither one of us can fly, so they'll naturally assume an assault from the ground. Rachman'll realize we've come in along the watercourse, 'stead of across the desert. He'll take note of the coverin' fire, figure one of us is about to rush the doors, or one of the ground-floor windows.'

'If it was me in there,' Santee said, squinting at the adobe, 'I'd've put the hostages well out of the way soon's I arrived. Out of the way means away from doors, and that means top floor. You say one man's up there now, but if those owlhoots come under attack, they'll want all guns to bear on the entrances.'

'Right. So when that happens they'll both make sure they're on the ground-floor, standin' well back from the door, ready to open up and blow off the head of the first man steps inside,' Buchanan said. 'Which brings us back to that lass rope. If we've got this figured right, your shots'll draw a burst of return fire, then whoever's up there'll rush downstairs to join his pard.' Buchanan's grin was bleak. 'Lower your aim. Pump slugs in through the ground-floor windows. At that same time, out back, I'll toss a loop over one of them high beams, start climbin'. Give me a few minutes, then yell for them fellers to come on out, hands up. They'll laugh in your face, so keep talkin', or keep shootin'. When I'm ready, I'll give a yell–'

'You're walkin' into a trap,' Santee protested.

'Maybe, but I'm gettin' me an extra man to help me tackle them desperadoes,' Buchanan said. 'He'll make good use of that Paterson you've been takin' such care of.'

'Harry Pepper?'

'Damn right.' Buchanan held out his hand, accepted the gleaming Colt Paterson Santee handed over with obvious reluctance. 'That gunny-sack they took from the bank and toted all this way's stuffed with money belonging to Harry's customers. If he wants to give it back to them, he'll use this pistol to–'

He got no further. The vicious crack of a rifle cut off his words. Alongside him, Josh Santee cursed, grabbed the Winchester and carton of shells and rolled into the choked canal. The slug snicked through branches, chopping twigs and showering Buchanan with dry leaves. He dropped flat, rolled on the baked earth, squinted up through the trees. A voice roared. It was followed by a woman's high-pitched scream. Then, chillingly, Wink Rachman's crazy laugh rang out over the cooling desert and his voice screamed out with maniacal venom.

'I've got you spotted, Josh Santee. Call up Tide Buchanan, let's get this all settled!'

A second shot blasted, then a third, slamming into the trees. But Santee was wriggling like a snake, down below the broken edge of the watercourse. Behind him, Buchanan wormed his painful way through the broken debris of untold centuries, grabbed hold of a kicking boot.

'Far enough!'

Santee stopped, twisted his head around, spat shreds of splintered bark as Buchanan wriggled alongside.

'This don't change nothing,' Buchanan told him. 'He saw you, not me.' He paused, breathing hard, face glistening. 'Drivin' us

167

down here's done us a favour, pushed me part way to where I want to go. Now all it needs is for you to keep them occupied....'

As if to reinforce his optimism, Rachman's harsh voice again shattered the stillness.

'If you're down there, Buchanan, you can forget all about rescuin' darlin' Beth and poor old Harry Pepper. Both of 'em're all trussed up where they can't be got at. So come on in like a man, make your play and....'

But as the escaped convict rattled on, bragging and blustering into the thin air, Buchanan was no longer listening. With Santee's Paterson tucked into his belt, the lass rope looped around his shoulder, he was off like a sidewinder along the water-course, hitching his way on hip and shoulder in order to keep below the level of the low wall. Behind him, Santee opened up with the Winchester and, as hot lead thunked into the adobe walls, Wink Rachman fell silent.

The talk was all done. It was time for action.

FIFTEEN

The steady thwack of Winchester bullets drilling into the adobe walls and the patter of plaster raining down on the mesquite accompanied Buchanan's sweating, panting progress along the dusty watercourse, the crack of the outlaws' returned fire suddenly sounding from almost directly overhead as he wriggled level with the adobe watchtower of Casa Grande, passed the corner of the building and was at once swallowed by the long shadows of evening.

From that point on he was able to breathe a mite easier, but not relax. It took another dozen powerful, bruising thrusts with his elbows before he could stop and roll, gasping, onto his back. For a few long seconds he listened, allowed himself a small smile as he heard the owlhoots' fire cease, then recommence. Only now the sound of the rifle was almost deafening, it was so close, and Buchanan closed his eyes in relief.

The gunman had come down from his

eyrie and, with his partner, was preparing to meet the attack from the ground.

Dashing the sweat from his eyes with his sleeve, Buchanan looked through the tangle of mesquite and let his gaze run up the ancient walls, squinting into the dazzling glare of the flaming evening skies.

The window he'd chosen for a way into the building was high, dark and empty. The hostages should be in that room. Both of the owlhoots were now on the ground floor, fully occupied by Josh Santee's measured, aimed shots. Everything was going according to plan. If Santee could keep up the pressure, if he didn't run out of shells....

Refusing to consider the alternative, Buchanan climbed to his feet, ripping himself free of the clinging thorns. In a sudden deathly silence as the deputy abruptly ceased firing, his booted foot rolled, sending a stone rattling. He toppled sideways, grabbed for the parapet, held his breath, waited for the shout of glee, the tremendous blow of the death-dealing slug.

Neither was forthcoming. Buchanan steadied himself, drew breath. Santee recommenced firing, spacing his shots now; probably, Buchanan guessed, conserving his ammunition. And with the realization that the boy's full magazine could well be his last, the marshal slipped the lass rope from his shoulder and shook its coils loose, took one swift glance overhead, then swung his arm back and snapped it forward to send a loop whirling towards a high, projecting beam.

The lass rope whispered as it uncoiled. The loop slipped neatly over the beam, slapped the wall, bounced – and with a prayer that was too fast for thought, Buchanan jerked it tight. He leaned back, put tension on the rope. The rawhide softly sang. Tide Buchanan grinned a savage grin.

He tore himself free of the mesquite, vaulted over the crumbling parapet and went up the rope hand over hand with his boots silent against the rough adobe walls and his body straining backwards. He worked his way past two glassless windows, caught snatched glimpses of time-worn wooden ladders in empty rooms where the red evening sun slanted; heaved himself onward and upward towards a window that was blurred by the stinging salt sweat trickling into his eyes.

Then, two-thirds of the way up, his upper hand slipped on the slick rawhide and he skidded helplessly down the wall. He slid a terrifying six feet, desperately clamped his hand on the thin leather and almost dislocated his shoulder as he jerked to a stop. Momentum flicked his feet off the wall. He hung vertically. His face was mashed against the adobe, smearing blood. Breath bubbled through his nostrils. His legs dangled like those of a man hanged. Eyes clamped shut, clinging on with one hand, he took a twisting turn of rawhide around his left wrist, let his body go limp. Gritting his teeth against the burning agony of a strained shoulder and rope-burned palm he forced himself to stillness while the fierce pumping of his heart gradually slowed.

When he found the strength and the will to go on he took just four, trembling, overhand pulls on the rope and his head bumped against the beam.

Seconds later his leg was over the window sill, and he had dropped soundlessly into the room.

'My God – Tide Buchanan!'

The salty taste of blood was in Buchanan's mouth as he leaped to Harry Pepper's side, plucking his knife from his boot. Two swift slashes of the razor-sharp blade severed the pigging string lashing the fat banker's wrists. A swift look into his eyes saw anger tinged bewilderment and something that was carefully hidden. Buchanan clapped him on the shoulder and, as Harry Pepper began rubbing circulation back into his hands, he placed the Colt Paterson on the boards alongside the banker, saw him nod and frown.

Then Buchanan turned to the other hostage.

Beth Carter was trussed like a turkey. Her face was pale, her dark hair mussed, but her eyes blazed fire and the look she bestowed on Tide Buchanan set his heart racing. He knelt by her, carefully cut through her rawhide bonds, helped her to sit up.

'This could get rough,' he said huskily. 'I want you to stay up here.'

'How many men?'

He grinned. 'Just me and Josh. And Harry.' He twisted his head, saw the banker up on his feet, pistol in hand, looking out of the window. 'But, hell, none of that matters now. The only problem was hostages. With you two free, Rachman and Torres are lost.'

'Be careful. That man, Charlie Rachman....' She reached up a hand and trailed her fingertips across his cheek, tenderly touched the abrasions where his face had scraped down the adobe wall. Her eyes softened. She said, 'After this, when all this is over and done, Tide Buchanan–'

The banker's excited cry broke through the promise in her softly spoken words.

'Josh Santee's taken a slug, gone down!'

'Goddamn!'

Buchanan squeezed the girl's hand then spun away. At the window, Harry Pepper pointed with a shaking hand to a break in the ragged line of stunted cottonwoods and trangled mesquite marking the path of the ancient watercourse. Josh Santee was flat on his back, arms flung wide. The front of his shirt was soaked with blood. As Buchanan watched, one leg twitched, and was still.

'They think I'm out there,' he said quietly, biting back anger because anger had no place in a fight. He turned away from the window, sickened. 'Let's show 'em they're wrong, Harry.'

The floors of the adobe of Casa Grande were linked by crude ladders that poked through square holes cut in the rough boards. The hatchways were in line, so that by peering over the lip of the top one, Buchanan was looking down into what, in the gathering gloom, appeared to be a bottomless pit: four ladders, with wide-spaced rungs worn smooth by moccasined

Indian feet, dropped clear to the ground floor. Those ladders were the only way down. They would need to be negotiated backwards, leaving the man on the ladder defenceless against a sudden burst of fire from below.

'I'll go first,' Buchanan said. 'You stand close with that pistol ready to plug anything that–'

'No!' Pepper barged heavily past Buchanan and teetered on the lip of the hatchway, the Paterson jutting from his plump fist. His face was flushed. The anger that had been in his eyes, that same anger that Buchanan was keeping firmly tamped down, had turned to a boiling rage that was driving the banker to recklessness.

'Step aside, Harry,' Buchanan said tersely. 'We do this together, there's no call for you to take risks.'

'Ain't there?' The banker's jaw jutted. With a metallic snick he cocked the big pistol. 'Those two bastards forced me out of my home, forced me to open the goddamn safe – forced me to ride out to this godforsaken hole toting a sackful of banknotes. By God, that's too much for one man to take!'

As Buchanan moved forwards, reaching for him, Harry Pepper caught the advancing marshal in the chest with a powerful, stiff-arm jab and quickly stepped back onto the ladder. Grunting, he lowered his bulk from one worn rung to the next, then another. His face gazed up at Buchanan, glistening with sweat. His eyes gleamed with triumph, but the fury was leaking away like sand and that triumph failed to hide the naked fear.

Another step down. His head drew level with the floor, sank below it. The ladder creaked, like the thin, wailing cry of an ailing cat. Dust drifted. Fragments of stone pattered on the wooden floor below.

Warily, certain that the sharp ears of the outlaws on the ground floor must have caught those sounds, Buchanan leaned forward to peer past the descending banker, saw the succession of dark hatchways yawning in the shadows; saw the ladder bowing under the big man's weight.

'Harry...' he cautioned – and could do nothing but watch with growing horror.

Again the ladder creaked and groaned as parched, ancient timbers took the unaccustomed strain; as old, inflexible, termite-infested wood was forced to flex.

The ladder broke with a tremendous, splintering crack.

Harry Pepper fell backwards, still clutching a rung that was now attached to nothing but the air through which he plummeted. His mouth gaped wide in a silent scream of fear. His eyes gleamed white in the gloom. He fell with his body tilting backwards from the vertical, dropped straight through the next hatchway and hit the edge a tremendous blow with the back of his head. His neck snapped. He was thrown violently forward against the next ladder, shattering dry rungs one after the other on his way down. This time the force of the impact tossed him backwards like a rag doll. He hit the next floor with his upper body on the boards, the edge of the hatchway at his waist, his hips and legs over the drop.

His back broke with a sickening snap.

Watching from above with his face a frozen mask of horror, Buchanan saw the broken body teeter, then slowly slide over the edge. What was left of Harry Pepper hit the hard dirt floor slackly, without life. Then, at last, the Colt Paterson was jolted from his grasp. It bounced high, and went off with a bang and a dazzling flash.

The slug hit stone, whined its way into a sudden, terrible silence.

SIXTEEN

'Buchanan!'

Beth Carter touched his shoulder as Wink Rachman's voice rang out, echoing hollowly from the ground floor of the old watchtower.

He took her hand, stepped back from the hatchway, put a finger to his lips.

'Buchanan, goddammit man, we know you're up there!' the outlaw yelled. 'Everybody knows the only man in Gila Bend packs a Paterson with a broken grip is Cole Santee's boy. But Josh Santee's lyin' in the scrub, bleedin' to death. There's only one way Harry Pepper could have got himself cut free of those ties and ended up on his back in the dirt holdin' the boy's pistol.'

'Stand-off?' Buchanan said quietly, looking into Beth Carter's troubled eyes. 'Harry wrecked the ladders. They can't get up here. I can't get down.'

'Oh, but you can, can't you?' Her faint smile was tremulous, but her eyes shone with faith. 'You came up a lass rope, and

178

that's the way you'll go down, and finish those two.'

'Some tricks only work the once,' he said, knowing that to go back the same way was suicide, knowing, too, that he was arguing against the inevitable. 'That rope's still dangling. They'll go lookin', figure out–'

'Pull it up,' Beth said with a meaning look. 'Now, quickly.'

Buchanan nodded, eyes suddenly alight with hope, his understanding instant. He took a breath, leaped across the room to the window, leaned out and left the loop secured to the beam but swiftly pulled in the thirty feet of slack rope. Even as he did so he heard pounding footsteps, jerked back inside as, far below, a man raced around the corner.

'This was for you,' he said with misgivings as he crossed the room with the rope and let the end drop through the hatchway, watched it fall to its length and hang twitching above Harry Pepper's body. 'God forbid, but if I was in trouble you could have taken your chance, gone out through the window–'

'There *is* no way out,' she said. 'There is no future for us, while those two are down there, waiting.' Again she touched him.

'Now, go, quickly.'

'What bothers me is there's more than one rope in the world,' Buchanan said. His hand slid to his boot, came up with his knife. 'If Torres decides to use his, climb up the same way I did while Rachman's got me occupied – cut the rope.'

At her nod, Buchanan left her holding the knife and sat on the edge of the hatchway, grasped the rope, twisted his body and slid into space. He went down fast, the rope hissing, his hands on fire. His boots slammed against the rough boards of the next floor. He fell, rolled, drew and cocked his Remington. Two floors down, Wink Rachman leaped out of the shadows, stood astride Harry Pepper. His six-gun roared flame. Slugs clipped the edge of the hatchway. Buchanan counted to three. Then he rolled to the edge of the hatchway and drove Rachman back with two fast, accurate shots.

Like greased lightning Tide Buchanan spun, pouched his six-shooter, dropped his legs over the lip. In that instant of swift movement a gun barked behind him and a slug sent sharp splinters singing. Cursing, he went over the edge, a snatched glance at the window revealing a swarthy gunslinger grinning savagely as he dangled on a rope and looked along the barrel of his six-shooter.

'Beth,' Buchanan roared. 'Watch out!'

Again the pistol cracked, spitting death at close range. But Buchanan was gone, slipping down the rope, the 'breed gunslinger deliberately blanked from his mind, his gaze now fixed on the square opening below him, the limp body of the banker. A broken rung snagged his shirt, spun him around. Another drew blood from his cheek. Still spinning, off balance, his boots hit the floor at the edge of the next hatchway, twisted on the lip, and for an instant it seemed that he would fall the remaining distance and land on the dead banker.

Then, arms windmilling, body arched, he fell backwards to the board floor.

But not fast enough.

Muzzle flame lit up the lower room, illuminated Pepper's dead countenance. Wink Rachman's slug clipped Buchanan's buckle as he fell backwards, seared a river of agony across his chest and clipped the lobe of his ear as he twisted his head aside.

Two floors above him, Beth Carter called out sharply, her voice pitched high with anger.

Somewhere, not too far distant, hoofbeats

sounded, and Buchanan grinned with relief as blood dripped onto his shoulder and trickled warmly under his belt, knowing that Josh Santee had made it to where the outlaws' horses were hitched.

It was too late to get help but, by hell, if the outlaws bested him, and lived, they'd be stranded, on foot, in the burning desert – and the boy could surely save his own skin!

The thought gave Tide Buchanan the strength he needed. He knew that Charlie 'Wink' Rachman was waiting for him, legs braced as he stood astride Harry Pepper, his six-gun cocked, pointing up towards the only place left for Buchanan to go.

Even as the thoughts sped through his mind, Rachman spoke up.

'This is the finish, Buchanan,' the crazy voice drawled. 'You put me away, now you'll pay. If you've got the guts – come all the way down and take what's comin'.'

'A man with guts,' Buchanan called, 'would put up his pistol, step outside, start this thing even.'

'Most of the men I know did that,' Rachman said, 'are pushin' up daisies in Boot Hills from here to Abilene.' He punctuated the words with a shot that splintered the boards alongside Buchanan's leg and howled all the way up to the roof.

And suddenly, the howl of that wayward hunk of hot lead was matched, and put to shame.

It started up high, trailed eerily down in a fading banshee wail past each of the glassless windows of the watchtower, and was cut off with a thump as Pedro Torres hit the ground.

In that instant, Tide Buchanan took his chance.

He went over the edge in a roll, releasing the rope. His deliberate fall took him down on top of a startled Wink Rachman who had half turned as his pard fell from the upper storey and wailed away his useless life. Buchanan knocked him flat. The outlaw fell back, kicking. Buchanan floundered. Sprawled across Harry Pepper's warm body, he tried to scramble to his feet and pull his six-gun and achieved neither. A flailing boot cracked against his wrist. The Remington flew from his hand. And as agony knifed through his arm and, blinded by pain, he groped feebly for the lost pistol, across from him, outlined against the wide open door that was backlit by the flaming ball of the setting sun, Wink Rachman was up, and ready.

The cocking of a pistol stopped Buchanan. On his knees, dishevelled, blood-stained, he straightened proudly.

'No chances, my friend,' Rachman said.

'None asked for,' Buchanan said hoarsely. The pistol rose, levelled.

'You've got time for a prayer.'

'Before you, that would be sacrilege.'

Rachman laughed without mirth. Darkly silhouetted against the sun, he settled his aim on the centre of Buchanan's chest. It seemed to Buchanan that the outlaw said something, hissing the words through clenched teeth. Then, as a shadow moved lazily against the sun and the seconds crawled like ants across a dying man's skin, a shot blasted, driving Buchanan backwards.

Wink Rachman seemed to snap in half. He went over backwards, bending in a way no man could bend, bleeding like a bull with its throat cut. When he hit the dirt floor, he twitched once, a scorpion with a broken back. Then he lay silent and still.

The man with the shotgun stepped across the threshold and said, 'In case you misheard, Tide, what Rachman said was, "You first Buchanan – then the judge".' Judge Ed Payne laughed. 'I put him away once, I've put him away a second time – only this one's for keeps.'

'I always knew you could ride, and shoot, Judge. When I told you where I was headed, I didn't expect you to follow.' He ripped off his bandanna, mopped blood from his face, said quietly, 'Maybe I was wrong, keepin' you in jail?'

'No, sir. Facing crazy outlaws is one thing, but Agnes Smallbone is something else entirely.'

'I heard your horse,' Buchanan said, climbing shakily to his feet and stepping over the bodies. 'Thought it was Josh, makin' a run for it.'

'The boy's dead,' Payne said.

'Him and his pa.' Buchanan shook his head sorrowfully. 'And Torres? I heard him call out as he fell, reckon Beth must've done like I told her.'

'Maybe she did.' Payne broke the shotgun, flicked out two smoking, empty cartridges, and Buchanan felt chilled as he realized the judge had let Rachman have both barrels. 'All I know is that outlaw outside's got your knife sticking out of the middle of his chest....' Payne broke off, thought for a moment, said slyly, 'Seems to me that girl and my Agnes Smallbone've got a lot in

185

common. Now, if you want to do some serious thinkin' before you act hasty and go down on one knee making promises and such–'

'Judge,' Buchanan cut in, grinning, 'you could have a point there. Beth can't get down, we can't get up, and I guess she's somewhat puzzled about what's goin' on. So why don't we do some clearin' up down here, let her reflect on the meaning of life, get herself in the right mood to welcome her rescuer with open arms.'

'Why don't we do that,' Ed Payne said with a broad wink.

The publishers hope that this book has given you enjoyable reading. Large Print Books are especially designed to be as easy to see and hold as possible. If you wish a complete list of our books please ask at your local library or write directly to:

Dales Large Print Books
Magna House, Long Preston,
Skipton, North Yorkshire.
BD23 4ND

This Large Print Book for the partially sighted, who cannot read normal print, is published under the auspices of

THE ULVERSCROFT FOUNDATION